The Impossible Lisa Barnes

The Anika Scott Series

#1 *The Impossible Lisa Barnes*
#2 *Tianna the Terrible*
#3 *Anika's Mountain*
#4 *Ambush at Amboseli*
#5 *Sabrina the Schemer*

The Impossible
Lisa Barnes

Karen Rispin

Tyndale House Publishers, Inc.
Wheaton, Illinois

Library of Congress Cataloging-in-Publication Data

Rispin, Karen, date
  The impossible Lisa Barnes / Karen Rispin.
     p.   cm. — (Anika Scott ; #1)
  Summary: Despite the urgings of her parents, twelve-year-old Anika finds it
difficult to befriend the obnoxious new girl who just moved from the United
States to Kenya.
  ISBN 0-8423-1614-0
  [1. Friendship—Fiction.   2. Behavior—Fiction.   3. Christian life—Fiction.]
I. Title.   II. Series: Rispin, Karen,, date
Anika Scott ; #1.
PZ7.R494Im   1992
[Fic]—dc20   92-19253

Printed in the United States of America

99   98   97   96   95
 8   7   6   5   4

For Mom and Dad

Chapter One

~~~~~~~~~~~~~~~~~~~~~~~~

I swallowed hard and knocked on the door.

Nothing happened. My stomach felt all twisted up as I knocked again. I hate meeting new people. This time was even worse than usual because I really wanted to be friends with Lisa Barnes. She was the only kid my age on our mission station.

The Barneses were a new missionary family. They had come to Africa while Sandy (that's my ten-year-old sister) and I were away at boarding school. Mom said that the Barneses had two kids, Alex and Lisa. Alex was eight years old and Lisa was twelve, like me. Now here I was, standing at their front door because Mom had sent me down to invite them for supper.

Finally the door opened, and a man with a bald head loomed over me. He was huge. Before I had a chance to say anything he boomed, "Now let me see. Who have we here? This little sweetie must be Anika Scott. Am I right?"

He stuck his hand out for me to shake. It was as big

as a Frisbee. *Little sweetie? Me? Ha!* I thought as my hand disappeared into his huge mitt.

"We've heard lots about you," he went on. "You're going to have to help our Lisa get used to Kenya." He was practically yelling in my face, like he thought I was half a mile away instead of right in front of him. "A sweetie pie like you shouldn't have any trouble with that, though," he boomed. Then he thumped me on the shoulder and laughed really loud. I cringed.

A thin woman with light brown hair in a ponytail came up behind him. "Now honey, let the poor child get a word in," she cooed. (No kidding! She really cooed! Just like a dove. Her voice was low and slow, almost like she was singing. I'd heard Southern accents before, but never anything as wild as this!)

Mr. Barnes didn't give me a chance to say anything. He kept right on bellowing. "I hear you kids call adults Aunt and Uncle, Anika. That would make me your Uncle Joey. And this here is your Aunt Elsie. Ha, ha, ha! It's a cute habit."

OK, so he was right. Missionary kids *do* call adults they know well Aunt and Uncle. But I didn't know these people—and right now I wasn't sure I wanted to. Mr. Barnes thumped me on the shoulder again, and I backed away.

Mrs. Barnes came after me and patted me on the

arm. "It's so nice to meet you, honeybunch," she cooed. "I'm sure you and Lisa will be wonderful friends. Once she gets to know you and y'all are friends, why, she'll like it here just fine."

I managed to say something about being glad to meet her, too, and then I remembered why I was there. "Um, we wanted to invite your whole family to our house for supper tonight. Would you be able to come?"

Mrs. Barnes gave a soft little scream and hugged me. I went stiff, but she kept on hugging anyway. "It's so kind of y'all to invite us," she said. "Now, can I bring anything along to help your mama?"

I said Mom hadn't said anything about that and got out of there as quickly as I could. Whew! What if Lisa turned out to be like her parents? I shook my head.

When I got back to the house, Mom was correcting papers in her office. She teaches Bible school.

"The Barneses said they'd come," I said as soon as I walked in. "I never even saw Lisa. Is she as weird as her parents?"

"Anika, be a little kinder," Mom said.

"Well, is she?" I asked again.

"I don't really know what Lisa is like," Mom said. "I've only seen her once, and then she looked like she'd been crying. Mrs. Barnes said that Lisa really didn't want to leave her friends in America. She's having trouble adjusting." Mom put her pencil down and looked at me thoughtfully. "I want you to make a special effort to make Lisa feel welcome. Be sure to reach out to her and be her friend."

"Mommmm," I really dragged it out. I hate being lectured, especially about things I already want to do.

"Now, Anika," Mom said, "don't you think that ploud wees Jesus?"

I burst out laughing. For some reason none of us have ever figured out, Mom is always getting her words all tangled up. We've gotten pretty used to it, though, and can usually figure out what she means.

In this case, I figured she meant to say that my making friends with Lisa would please Jesus. Mom always brings everything back to pleasing God. I think she's memorized half of the Bible. Sometimes that can be a real pain. Most of the time I don't mind, though. It makes me feel kind of safe.

After I left Mom, I climbed to my favorite thinking branch in the mango tree just by our front porch. I know, twelve is a little old for tree climbing, but for as long as I can remember I'd always come to sit on this branch whenever I was worried. This time I brought the book I was reading with me, but I was already almost at the end of it, so it didn't take me long to finish it.

I pulled a dead leaf off of the branch above me and

thought about Lisa. *How could anyone not want to live in Kenya? I wouldn't give up being a missionary kid for anything!*

That made me think of the other thing that was worrying me. If Daddy didn't get all the way better soon, I might *have* to give up being a missionary kid. No more camping in the game parks, no more trips to the coast, no more mango tree. It meant exile to the boring, smoggy U.S.A., where the only thing to do was fry your brain watching reruns on TV. (At least, that's how I thought of it.)

Daddy had caught hepatitis. That's a disease you get from dirty water and stuff. He had gotten it at a training conference at Thika for African church leaders. He was mostly better, but he wouldn't rest and get all the way better. In two days we were leaving for the coast so he could rest. That was OK with me because the Indian Ocean is my very favorite place in all the world. I don't worry about anything there. It's that kind of place.

I wasn't there yet, though, and I was plenty worried now. I shifted on my branch, then heard voices coming toward our house. There was no mistaking that loud voice or that soft, slow one, either: the Barneses were coming. I tried to peer through the leaves to see what Lisa looked like, but the heavy, dark green leaves were too thick for that. I'd already seen Lisa's little brother,

Alex, out playing with David Stewart, one of the kids from another missionary family. The Stewarts had two kids, Traci, who was ten, and David, who was nine. Traci and my sister Sandy were best friends.

Anyway, when I saw Alex, he had seemed pretty normal. Maybe Lisa would be OK, too.

I guess I'd better get down there, I thought without much enthusiasm. I started to slide down the branch I was on when I noticed a chameleon out near the top of the branch above me. There were chameleons everywhere on the station. This one matched the bark exactly and was about as long as my hand. Like all three-horned chameleons, it looked like a tiny, skinny triceratops. You know, the dinosaur with three horns.

Hey great, I thought. *I can show it to Lisa.* I really like animals; they're neat. Sure, I knew that not everybody liked them as much as me, but most kids were interested—especially in chameleons.

I stood up slowly, balanced myself on the branch I'd been sitting on, and caught the chameleon gently. One of its eyes was looking at me, a tiny bright beady dot in a round bump of wrinkled skin. The other eye was still looking at something up in the dark green leaves.

It twisted its body and opened its mouth at me. It looked fierce, but chameleons are really very gentle. You can keep them in a box and watch them catch flies with their superlong tongues. Or you can just let them walk on you. We always let them go after a day or so.

At least Mom won't be able to say I'm not trying to be friends, I thought. I slid backwards down the long, smooth gray branch, carefully holding the chameleon in my hand.

When I got down on the ground all the Barneses were on the front porch with Mom and Daddy and Sandy. The kids were kind of eyeing each other, and the adults were talking. I walked up and stood by Sandy. The chameleon was on my shirt now, just holding on.

Lisa was taller than me; she already looked like a teenager. She had light brown hair and clothes that were really in style. I had on my usual old shorts and T-shirt. I wished I'd cleaned up and put some other clothes on, not that I had anything half as nice as her clothes.

I was just going to say hi when Lisa started screaming bloody murder and pointing at me like I was Count Dracula or something.

"What is it? What is it? Take it away!" she howled.

Sandy and I just stared at her. What on earth was her problem? Then I realized she must be talking about the chameleon. I took it off my shirt and backed up. By now all the grown-ups were staring at me, too.

I turned to Mom, kind of holding out the chameleon.

She was standing right by Mrs. Barnes—who suddenly started screaming, too. She screamed even higher than Lisa. Daddy took two quick steps toward me, picked me up by my elbows, and carried me off the porch. I just about died.

"What do you think you're playing at, Anika Gail Scott?" he demanded. "Scaring guests is an obnoxious trick." He was kind of panting from moving fast—that made me feel even worse.

"Honest, Daddy, I didn't mean to. I was going to give it to Lisa. I thought she'd like it."

He just stared at me like he couldn't believe his ears. I was tired of being stared at, so I just looked down and held still. I noticed that my blue thongs were getting too small. My feet were kind of dusty, too, and there was a big smear of red dirt across my left foot. I rubbed it on the back of my leg.

Daddy sighed like he was very tired. "Well, put the chameleon down and come in and apologize. And next time, think a little harder." He walked back into the house.

Daddy's always saying that, about thinking first. I really felt dumb because he was right. Like, I know Mrs. Jantz at school is afraid of chameleons, and so are a couple of other air-headed women. I should have guessed Lisa would be like that.

"Stupid, stupid, stupid," I muttered through

clenched teeth as I stuck the chameleon on the trunk of the mango tree.

For a second I thought about climbing into the safe green dome of the mango tree and just staying there till the Barneses left. But I knew it wouldn't help. It would just get me into more trouble.

I dragged my feet slowly through the soft red dust of the driveway. On the veranda, I curled my toes up tight to keep my thongs from making noise.

"I don't believe she meant to scare you," Daddy was saying. Lisa was still kind of hiccuping from crying.

I walked in and everybody stared at me again. My face felt hot, and my tongue seemed to be too big for my mouth.

"Ah, I'm sorry," I blurted. "I wanted it to be a surprise."

Mr. Barnes started laughing and boomed, "It sure was."

Then all the other grown-ups laughed, too, even Mom and Daddy. I wanted to run, but that would only make it worse.

"Come and sit down, honey," said Mrs. Barnes. "We forgive you, only don't make it quite so much of a surprise next time. You'll have to tell us sometime what that creature was."

I slid into my chair next to Sandy. Sandy looked at me and kind of raised one eyebrow, signaling toward Mrs. Barnes and Lisa.

All through the meal Mr. Barnes and especially Alex, who was eight, quizzed us about chameleons and the other animals that are around. Lisa never said a thing.

I kept on looking at her, but she just looked down. I'd sure blown my chance of ever being friends. But then, how *could* we be friends? She seemed to hate everything I liked: Kenya, animals—everything. Besides, she looked about six years older than me. I sighed.

We'd just started on the dessert when Daddy said something that made me stop eating entirely. Even loquat pie, which is my very favorite dessert, didn't taste good any more.

"Well, Joey," he said. "Have you made your decision about coming to the coast with us?"

"You bet your boots," boomed Mr. Barnes. "We're looking forward to swimming in a genuine tropical ocean."

Sandy and I looked at each other, horrified. How dare Daddy invite somebody to the coast with us without even telling us? Especially somebody like the Barnes family.

Mr. Barnes was still talking. "It sure ought to get Lisa to quit moping and see what a great little continent Africa is. Right, Lisa?" and he poked her hard in the ribs.

Suddenly, I actually felt sorry for Lisa.

As soon as the Barneses left, Sandy yelled, "Daddeeee, why did you have to go and invite the Barneses?"

"Yeah. At least you could have asked us first. It's not fair!" I added.

"We didn't ask you first because you were away at school. Also, we didn't know if the Barneses could come since they just got settled here. After all the packing up and moving, plus three months of language school, we thought they could use the break. Besides, we thought Anika would enjoy having somebody her own age there."

I squirmed. The coast is supposed to be a place where you don't have to worry, and the idea of spending time with Lisa Barnes made me nervous. I had a hard enough time keeping up with kids my age at school. I don't mean in schoolwork—that's OK. I mean in doing the right things, you know, socially. I never get it right. Now I was stuck with someone who looked ultrasophisticated and already hated me. Yuk.

Then I thought of something else. Daddy was supposed to rest and get better. I had him for sure this time.

"Daddy, we can't take them," I blurted. "How can you rest up with Mr. Barnes booming all over everyone? Even Bilge Water won't be restful with them there."

Bilge Water is the house we rent at the coast. It belongs to a Pakistani family. It's sort of like a cottage at the lake, and the family rents it out for not too much money. It's at the end of a long line of houses, each about a quarter of a mile apart and surrounded by thick bush. Anyway, the other houses are called things like the Cairns or Sea Breezes. I guess the people who built our house got sick of looking at supersweet names. Just to be different, they called their place Bilge Water— which is what you call the ucky water that sloshes around in the bottom of a boat. Don't let the name fool you, though. Bilge Water is one of the nicest places I know.

"Joey Barnes won't stop me from resting. He'll be another hand to help with any heavy work."

"It's not fair," Sandy practically yelled.

"Yeah!" I said. "Mr. Barnes talks so loud all the time, and Mrs. Barnes keeps gushing all over us—"

"Anika, I don't like your attitude one little bit," Mom interrupted, as if I was the only one complaining. "You're just thinking about yourself. I thought you memorized Philippians 2:4. 'Think not of your own interests, but also the inthers of otherests.'"

Daddy burst out laughing and said, "Yes, we really mustn't forget the 'inthers of otherests.' Now off to bed with you."

I lay in bed and thought about it. You'd never believe how good your very own bed feels when you usually have to sleep on squeaky boarding-school bunk beds. The wall beside my bed at home is made out of cinder blocks. It's always warm when I get in bed because the sun shines on it all afternoon. With my back up against the warm wall and my very own quilt over me, things didn't seem so bad after all. I still worried about Daddy not getting enough rest at the coast with the Barneses there, though.

"Dear Jesus," I prayed, "please make them not come with us."

That prayer kind of stuck to the roof of my mouth, so I stopped.

"Hey, Anika," Sandy whispered. Her bed is right across from mine. "Remember how Lisa was scared of that chameleon? I bet we could get them not to come if we kept telling them about all the big bugs and stuff at the coast."

It was an absolutely brilliant idea, even if Sandy did think of it. Still, I didn't answer right away. It really was brilliant . . . but it made me feel squirmy inside.

"What if Mom and Daddy find out?" I finally asked.

"We wouldn't be lying or anything."

Sandy was right. There are more huge bugs, snakes, and spiders at the coast than anywhere else in Kenya.

Besides, if Lisa and her mom were screeching all the time, Daddy wouldn't be able to rest. At least that's what I told myself. I just hated it when Daddy looked so tired. Everything was different with him sick.

"What if a lizard fell on Mrs. Barnes?" Sandy said all of a sudden and started giggling like mad. I don't think Sandy was as worried about Daddy as I was. At least she acted like she hardly noticed that there was anything different about him.

"Shhh, Mom will hear you."

"What is it? What is it? Take it away!" She screeched in a whisper, copying Lisa.

A picture of Mrs. Barnes hopping up and down with a lizard in her hair flashed into my head. I started giggling, too.

"Girls, settle down now," Daddy called.

I stuffed my pillow over my face, but I couldn't quit giggling. Every time I did stop, I'd see the look on Mrs. Barnes's face and start all over again. Or Sandy would start to giggle, and that would make me laugh too.

My tummy muscles were really sore from giggling by the time we finally got to sleep.

"Anika! Anika, wake up," Sandy was shaking me. I unglued my eyes, but I couldn't see a thing. It was pitch black out.

"Come on, wake up," she hissed at me in a whisper. "The Stewarts are downstairs, and there's something going on."

I couldn't hear David or Traci Stewart, but I could hear Uncle Paul Stewart's voice—and Aunt Bea Stewart was crying.

We went to the top of the stairs to listen.

"KLM flies to Amsterdam every Thursday. That's tomorrow," Daddy was saying. "You should be able to get a flight on to New York from there without too much trouble."

"But what about the kids?" Aunt Bea said, still crying.

"Now, don't worry about Traci and David," Mom said. "They'll do just fine with us."

What on earth was going on? I edged further down the stairs to hear better. Sandy followed.

"But you need to rest, Kevin," said Uncle Paul. I don't want to, but perhaps I should let Bea go home alo—"

"No! Your place is at your wife's side," Daddy interrupted. "The kids will be no trouble at all at the coast with us."

Sandy clapped her hands silently, then with a big grin on her face she practically dragged me back to our room. As soon as we were there, she started dancing around.

"Traci's coming to the coast with us! Traci's coming to the coast with us!" she whispered.

"Shhh, they'll hear you." I interrupted her mad dance. "Did you hear why Aunt Bea is crying?"

"Her mom's really sick or something. Anyway, they have to go back to the States, and Traci's coming to the coast with us!" She started dancing around again.

"I noticed," I said. It seemed like Sandy never cared about anything but herself. Here Aunt Bea is crying, and Daddy will have to put up with more kids, and all Sandy can do is dance around the room.

Suddenly she stopped dancing. "Hey, maybe Traci can help us scare the Barneses off."

"Yeah, maybe," I said really slowly, thinking the idea over. At least if the Barneses didn't come, Daddy could get some rest.

Chapter
Two

~~~~~~~~~~~~~~~~

"Anika, wake up." Sandy was shaking me again. "Let's go over and help Traci pack."

It took a second before I remembered: Traci and David Stewart were coming to the coast with us—and so were the Barneses. I cringed. Lisa Barnes would probably spend the whole three weeks looking down her sophisticated nose at me. I pulled the covers over my head.

Sandy yanked at them and said, "Come on. Get up! We have to tell Traci the plan."

Oh yes, the plan, I thought. *It just might work. At least there's a chance we can scare them off.* I stuck my head out and said, "OK, OK, I'm getting up."

Sandy took off downstairs, but Mom made her wait for me. She also made us clean our room first.

When we finally made it to Traci's room, Sandy blurted out, "I've got this super plan. If we get enough big bugs we can scare the Barneses into not coming."

"What are you talking about?" Traci demanded. She

has this dark red hair that's really long, and she flips it over her shoulder with a jerk when she asks questions.

I interrupted, "Traci, I'm sorry your grandma is sick."

"Oh, Dad said God will take care of her," Traci said. She didn't seem very worried. I guess Traci had only seen her grandmother a couple of times, and that was ages ago. "She never sends us presents as good as 'Nam Stewart sends, anyway," Traci added. "I don't see what the big fuss is about. I wish Mom and Dad weren't going, though."

"At least you get to come to the coast with us," Sandy said. "Only trouble is, the Barneses are coming, too."

"They're not! Dad never said that," Traci insisted.

"They are. They said so at supper last night," I said.

"Well, I don't want them. I just want to be with you guys."

"That's what I was talking about," said Sandy. "I've got a plan that'll make sure they won't come."

When she explained it, I felt all squirmy inside again. Traci, on the other hand, thought it was great.

"We could get your mom to invite them over for tea this afternoon," she said. "Then we could get started telling them all about all the snakessssss and lizzzards and tarraaaaantulas at the coast."

In Kenya, the grown-ups all have tea twice a day,

18

kind of like a coffee break. It's a British tradition that everybody in Kenya follows. *Having tea* doesn't just mean tea, though. There's usually cookies or something to munch on, too.

"Come on, let's go ask," said Sandy. "We can pack up after tea."

When we asked Mom if the Barneses could come to tea that morning, she looked at us very hard and said, "I'm glad you've had a change of heart." We tried to look innocent. Sandy tried so hard she looked really silly. Mom must have suspected something, but she said we could invite them. She had to go help the Stewarts pack up that morning, but they'd be gone by afternoon.

We'd just gotten back to the Stewarts' house when we heard an awful noise. It was coming from where Uncle Paul was backing their car out of the driveway. He stopped the car in a hurry and got out. We were all staring at the car when Alex Barnes and David came up.

"What's the matter Uncle Paul? Does your car sound funny?" asked Alex, and then he started to giggle.

"I don't see what's so funny," said Traci.

"Yeah, how would you feel if your car broke down just before you had to leave for the States?" Sandy demanded. She always stands up for Traci.

"It's not broken," said Alex, still giggling. "Dad just put stones in the hubcaps."

Uncle Paul kind of sighed, then he asked David to go get a screwdriver. Alex went with him.

"Why did Mr. Barnes do that?" asked Traci as soon as Alex was gone. I couldn't figure it out either. It seemed like a really stupid thing for a grown-up to do.

"Mr. Barnes believes practical jokes help people become friends. As he puts it, they 'break the ice and liven things up,'" said Uncle Paul.

I could practically hear Mr. Barnes booming that out in a fake-cheerful voice. *At least he could have left the Stewarts alone, with Aunt Bea's mom sick and everything,* I thought. Then I remembered he wouldn't have known yesterday when he did it. Maybe he still didn't know.

Then I had another thought: Mr. Barnes would probably be playing practical jokes the whole time we were at the coast, too. Ugh! I guess Sandy was thinking the same thing because she said, "Come on. Let's get going," and we headed for the Barneses' house to make sure they'd come to tea.

"We'd be just delighted, honey," Mrs. Barnes cooed. Then she reached for Traci, grabbed her arm, and started patting her. "Alex just told us about your grandma, Traci honey. You must be feeling absolutely terrible. Make sure you tell your mommy to call me if she needs any help with her packing."

Traci stood stiff as a stick. Mrs. Barnes probably thought that meant Traci was worried about her grandmother, because she bent over and hugged her.

As soon as we got out of there, Traci said, "I think we need a better plan."

"Hey, you guys, what about ani-ngongos?" I blurted out. Ani-ngongo was the name we called millipedes. I think it came from the Kikamba word for them. They have round, shiny black bodies and tiny red legs that go along in waves right under their bodies, so they look kind of like tiny trains.

"Well, what about them?" asked Sandy.

"You know the ones at the coast are about ten times bigger than the ones here. What if we catch a couple of the ones around here and tell them that?"

Sandy started to giggle. "What is it? What is it? Take it away!" she screeched.

Traci looked at Sandy confused, so she told Traci about what happened last night. I was still kind of embarrassed about it, but it *was* funny.

"That was a great idea, Anika, taking Lisa a chameleon," said Traci. "We've got to think of something even better."

"But I didn't do it to be mean," I said, a little frustrated. "I was trying to be nice."

"Yeah, sure," said Traci. "Anyway, let's look for ani-ngongos."

Then I giggled and blurted, "I know what we can call this plan— Bugging the Barneses."

"All right!" said Traci, "Let's get bugging!"

We forgot all about packing and started to look for our multilegged cohorts.

It's funny, but if you're looking for something it's almost impossible to find it. Usually we just sort of accidentally noticed ani-ngongos. Everywhere. Now we couldn't find any.

We looked all over the park—an open grassy place that's in the center of all the houses on station—and on the edges of the roads. We even poked around the flower gardens, but there were no ani-ngongos. Mrs. Barnes came out front when we were down near their house, so we tried to look innocent—but she'd only come out to call Alex home.

By now I was hot and tired and sorry I'd ever thought about ani-ngongos.

"Let's get David to help us," said Traci. "He's good at catching stuff. Alex isn't with him now."

We finally found David in the avocado tree behind Daddy's office, but he wouldn't help when we told him what it was for.

"No, I don't want to," he said. "I like Alex, even if his parents are kind of weird." David is a very determined person, so that was that.

"Don't you tell on us then!" Traci said in a kind of fierce voice.

I wasn't too worried, though. David probably wouldn't tell. If there is one thing you learn at boarding school, it's not to tattle. Tattletales are the lowest of the low.

He just looked disgusted. "Mom asked me if you were packed. Are you?"

We stared at each other for a minute, then headed back to the Stewarts' house in a hurry. Wouldn't you know it, just when we'd quit looking, Sandy found an ani-ngongo. Curled up tight in her palm (they always do that when you scare them), it didn't look like it could possibly scare anybody. But we took it back with us to the Stewarts' anyway.

"OK," said Traci, as she stuck the ani-ngongo in a matchbox. "We've got to figure out the best way to use this." Then she started hauling out her clothes and stuffing them in the suitcase Aunt Bea had put out.

"If we had a whole bunch we could stick them all over the room. Then when they notice them, we can say how much bigger the ones at the coast are," Sandy said.

"Well, we only have one," I said. "What if we sneak it into Mrs. Barnes's saucer?"

"What is it? What is it? Take it away!" screeched Traci, acting as though she was terrified of the pair of shorts she was packing. Everybody giggled.

"That won't work," Sandy interrupted, sitting up suddenly. "Mom would know that somebody had put it there. Besides, it might even get Barnabas in trouble."

Barnabas is our worker. He does cooking and cleaning and stuff. All the families on station have workers—even the African families like the Mitarus. Mr. Mitaru is Daddy's partner at the office.

"It won't get Barnabas in trouble," I said without thinking.

"It will, too. Mom will think he didn't check to see if the cups were clean when he put them out."

"Well, if he gets in trouble we'll just say it was us," I said.

"Then what's the use of doing it, if we just get in trouble?" said Sandy, plopping onto the end of Traci's bed.

"We could let it crawl on the floor and then all of a sudden pretend to notice it," I said.

"Well, OK," Sandy finally agreed.

"That's not very scary," said Traci, sounding disgusted.

"It will be if we tell the stories right," I said. "Maybe

we get on the subject, even the adults will join in telling stories about bugs and snakes and stuff at the coast. That should really bug Lisa and her mom."

"Like the time a snake was on your pillow," said Sandy, "and you came running out going, 'Sna! Sna! Sn'—"

I didn't like being reminded of that—I'd looked pretty dumb—so I interrupted. "Or the time you sat on a fire ant and cried all afternoon."

Sandy frowned, but Traci was started now, "Or the time the monitor lizard jumped off the top of the shower at Mom. Wow! Can you imagine what would happen if one did that to Lisa or Mrs. Barnes?" She stuffed her swimsuit in the suitcase, then sat on it, giggling.

Everybody was still giggling when the Stewarts' worker called, *"Chakula tayari."*

That's Swahili for "The food is ready." There are lots of different languages in Kenya. The people around our station talked Kikamba. Other tribes talk Kikuyu or Masai. White people talk English, Danish, French, or whatever. Indian people talk Hindi or Urdu. But all the different groups talk to each other in Swahili, which is called a trade language. The only people who talk Swahili at home, the Swahilis, live at the coast. We kids knew enough Swahili to get by.

"Well," I said, "time for Sandy and me to go home for lunch, too."

"Think up more good bugging stories," Traci called as we left.

After lunch, Sandy and I had to bring the wash in off the line and fold the towels and stuff. Sandy took off right away for Traci's house, but I wanted to read because I'd just started a new book.

I'd only read two pages when Daddy walked in. "Anika, I need some help stuffing and stamping some envelopes. I want you to come down to the office with me."

At first I wanted to say no. If I went down to the office I might miss tea with the Barneses. Then I remembered that if I helped, maybe Daddy would get more rest.

"OK, I'm coming," I called and threw my book down. I like helping Daddy in the office anyway. It always makes me feel like I'm part of something worthwhile. Still, I didn't want to miss tea.

I tried to hurry through the envelope stuffing, but the paper wouldn't fold straight. So I kept having to start over. I got some of the stamps on kind of crooked, and Daddy scolded me when he came to look.

"Daddeeee!" I said kind of irritated. "Why are we doing this anyway? Why don't you just rest and get better? I'm sick of these dumb envelopes."

"Anika, if I was just doing work for myself it would be one thing. But I feel that we're doing God's work. If I'm here in Kenya and can't do what God wants me to do, what good am I?"

"Yeah, but it makes you sicker," I muttered under my breath. It really bugged me when he wouldn't quit working and rest.

He just looked at me kind of sad, which made me feel bad. I sighed and put the stamps on more carefully.

The metal roof made popping sounds in the sun, and the office smelled of dust and books. Daddy's computer printer zipped loudly back and forth. I thought the job would never be done.

Just when I was ready to give up, Mom walked in.

"Well, they're off," she said. "I just hope Bea's mom recovers."

"Oh no!" said Daddy, slapping his forehead. "I meant to see them off. What time is it?"

"Tea time. The kids asked the Barneses over. Why don't you come up to the house for tea and take a break?" Mom suggested.

"I've got to get this done before we leave for the coast," Daddy said.

"Kevin, please take a break. You really mustn't work so hard. Joey Barnes will be there."

"I'm sorry, Hazel, I just can't afford to come

right now. I need Anika's help to finish that mailing, too."

"Daddeee, please," I burst in. "I've been working for ages already. Let's go."

"I do need that mailing done today."

"I know, Sandy and I can come down after supper and do it. If she won't come, I'll do it by myself. I promise. Please?" I begged.

"Why don't we all come down here after supper?" Mom asked. "That way we could work together."

Daddy said that would be OK, especially since he was planning to come down anyway, but he still didn't have time for tea. We just couldn't win.

Mom and I walked up across the park to our house. Neither of us was very happy. We were going to have tea on the porch, and when we got there, all four of the Barneses were already there. So were Traci and David. Sandy was playing gracious hostess.

Traci was sitting on the wide railing near the porch entrance. When I walked past, she stuck the matchbox in my hand. I tried to give it back, but she wouldn't take it. The adults were starting to look at us, so I had to keep it.

Mom brought out some milk to fill up a pitcher.

"Those little triangular milk packs are kinda cute," said Mr. Barnes. "I hate to say it, but they just don't

keep milk as fresh as the cartons we use in California.
It just doesn't taste right."

I grimaced. *He's always saying how awful Kenya is
compared to the States. If he liked it so much in the
U.S.A.,* I thought, *why didn't he stay there?*

"Well, at least it isn't full of growth hormones and
drugs," I said without thinking. Daddy had told us
about an article he'd read in *Time* magazine. It had said
a lot of American farm animals are fed loads of drugs.

Mom frowned at me and quickly changed the subject
to the Bible school. Traci walked over to sit by me. She
sort of jerked her head at my hand, but I didn't want to
drop the ani-ngongo yet. I tried to give it back to her.

Mr. Barnes noticed. "What have you girls got there
that's so interesting?" he boomed.

Traci and I just sat there.

"What have you got, Traci?" Mom asked.

"I don't have anything."

Great! She was leaving all the blame on me.

"Anika?" Mom said, her voice firm.

"Um, it's an ani-ngongo we found."

"An aunty who?" boomed Mr. Barnes. "I never met an
aunty that fit in a matchbox." He bellowed with laughter at his own joke.

I just couldn't stand the idea of him at the coast with
us, so I blurted out, "It's a centipede. A little one, see?"

and held my hand right under his nose. "The ones at the coast are ten times as big."

He wasn't scared at all. He grabbed my hand and held it open to look closer. The ani-ngongo uncurled and walked over onto his finger, and he just watched.

To make it worse, Alex came tearing over to him.

"Hey, neat, Dad. Can I have it? Let me hold it. OK?"

Mr. Barnes tried to put it onto Alex's hand, but it curled up and dropped onto the floor. Alex grabbed it and tried to uncurl it with his fingers.

"Don't! You'll break it," I yelled. "You have to hold still until it uncurls itself." I can't stand it when anything gets hurt, even bugs.

Alex stopped and stared at it.

"Are these things really ten times bigger at the coast?"

"Yes." It was Sandy, trying to get things back on track. "All the bugs are. There was a big, gold spider behind the house last year with a web five feet across."

Mrs. Barnes laughed kind of nervously. "I'm sure you girls are exaggerating."

"No, we aren't," said Traci. "One time there was a whole bunch of dead spiders in the coffee pot. A wasp stuffed the perking part full of dead spiders and mud, didn't it Aunt Hazel? Another time when my dad tried to kill a poisonous snake that was in the roof, it came right after him. He barely killed it in time."

Mrs. Barnes looked so horrified that for a second I thought our plan was working. Then Alex had to butt in.

"All right! Monster bugs!"

He had this huge grin on his face. With his big front teeth and mouse-colored hair sticking up, he looked like a crazy rat.

"I guess we'll have to get used to it sometime, seeing as God sent us over here," Mrs. Barnes said quietly.

That took all the fun out of it.

All of a sudden there was a loud screech. Alex had stuck the ani-ngongo on Lisa's head. The ani-ngongo fell off when Lisa jumped up, but she ran off the porch anyway. Mr. Barnes called her, but she ignored him and walked off, her back stiff.

Watching Lisa walk away, I felt a little bit sorry for her.

Mr. Barnes got up and walked over to Mrs. Barnes. He put one of his huge hands on her shoulder, then he looked up. "I'm sorry for Lisa and Alex's behavior. I guess they could learn a thing or two from your children."

Wow, I thought, *he sure doesn't know us very well.*

Mr. Barnes was still talking, "If Elsie, here, feels that the bugs and things at the coast would be too hard on her," he was rubbing Mrs. Barnes's shoulder, "or too hard on Lisa, then we'll just give it a pass." He looked down at Mrs. Barnes. "How about we let them know tomorrow morning? That should still give us time to pack up if we do decide to go."

Mom was agreeing that this would be fine when Traci kicked me in the shins and grinned. Then Sandy and Traci took off. I followed them.

As soon as we quit running, Sandy practically yelled, "It's working! It's working! Bugging the Barneses is working."

"Shhhh! They'll hear you," hissed Traci.

So we started running again.

We stopped near Daddy's office and plopped down under a cape chestnut tree. It's one of my favorite trees because it has these big purple flowers that look kind of like orchids.

"Mrs. Barnes still might decide to come," I said. "She did say that she has to get used to stuff."

"I bet your mom is telling them how great the coast is right now," said Traci glumly. "They'll never stay home after that."

"Then we'll just have to make sure they don't come," I said. I was thinking about Daddy again, but somehow I didn't want to say so. Since he had gotten sick, I'd hardly ever said anything about it to other kids. It's like it was too private or something.

"How?" demanded Sandy.

"We could do something to their car," I said.

"No way!" Sandy broke in. "Daddy would kill us. Besides, we don't know how."

"We wouldn't have to wreck their car or anything," I said, "We could just do something like Mr. Barnes did to your car, Traci. That would be fair."

"That's dumb," said Sandy. "Mr. Barnes probably knows all the practical jokes in the world."

"How about sticking a tarantula under the door when they're having supper?" asked Traci.

Sandy giggled and said, "Remember how Mom acted when that one came under our door last year?"

"It won't work," I said. "We don't know where to catch a tarantula, and, anyway, I don't really want to touch one. I bet you don't, either."

"OK, if you're so smart, what *should* we use then?" asked Sandy. She was trying to get under my skin, but I wasn't going to let her. We just had to make this work for Daddy.

I was staring out at the park, and I noticed two locusts over by the path.

"How about those?" I asked.

Locusts are giant grasshoppers that only come around once in a while. They are the same insects as the ones God sent as a plague on Egypt in the Bible. The locusts in Kenya come from the desert up north. Just like the Bible locusts, they used to cause real plagues, darken the sky, and eat up all the plants. Now people in airplanes sprayed the huge swarms, so they didn't cover the ground anymore. But there were still quite a few of them.

"Well, maybe if we caught a whole bunch and put them in their house . . . ," said Sandy, sounding kind of doubtful.

"Hey, I know," said Traci. "David was making a cage for locusts yesterday—you know how he likes bugs and making stuff. Maybe he still has them out in the shed. A big bunch of bugs like that should really bug Lisa and her family."

Just then Mom called us for supper. I suddenly remembered that we couldn't come out to help after supper, because we'd have to help Daddy. Traci didn't have to help at the office, though. When she had found out about all of us working at the office, she'd asked if she could stay home and read. Mom had said yes. David was going to have supper with the Barneses, because he and Alex were already friends.

Traci wasn't happy about having to get the locusts into the Barneses' house by herself. We made her promise to try, though.

"I don't see how we can do it now," she said. "They'll all be home for supper in a minute."

"Maybe you can get the bugs in through the kitchen door while they're eating supper," I said. "Their worker should have gone home by now."

"They don't have a worker," Traci interrupted.

"What?" I could hardly believe my ears. Everybody had workers.

"They don't believe in it," said Traci, sounding really sarcastic.

Mom called us again, so we had to quit talking and run home for supper. During the meal, Sandy and Traci kept looking at each other so much that Mom noticed and said they both looked like the cat that swallowed the cream.

"They're just excited about going to the coast," I said quickly, and "Traci is worried about her grandma."

Traci started to say, "I am not," but I kicked her on the shin, so she shut up. I could tell Mom was going to ask more, so I quickly asked Daddy what work he had to get done at the office. Daddy always likes to talk about what needs to be done.

As Daddy talked, I glanced at Traci and Sandy and smiled to myself, thinking about the locusts. Project Bugging the Barneses was about to take a giant leap forward!

Chapter Three

~~~~~~~~~~~~~~~~~~~~~~~~~~~~~~~~~~~

At the office, Sandy was folding letters, and I was stuffing them into envelopes. She handed me a letter and
whispered, "Do you think Traci will do it?"

"I don't know, she's *your* friend," I whispered back. I
halfway hoped she wouldn't. Sometimes bugging the
Barneses seemed like a really great idea. But other
times, it made me feel weird inside. Still, Daddy just
had to rest!

It was dark by the time we got done at the office.
Mom, Daddy, Sandy, and I were on our way across the
park when there was an incredible screech, and Mrs.
Barnes came tearing out of the front door of their house.

She was kind of hopping up and down and swatting
at her shoulder. Mr. Barnes was trying to keep up with
her. It looked like some crazy new kind of square dance.

"What on earth?" said Mom. She and Daddy hurried
over to see what was going on. I held back. If you're too
close to things, it's easier to get blamed. I guess Sandy
felt the same way, because she stayed with me.

By the time they'd gotten the locust off of Mrs. Barnes, the Mitarus were there, too. Mrs. Barnes sure can scream. Traci turned up next to Sandy just when Mrs. Barnes finally got quiet.

All the adults were in a little huddle around Mrs. Barnes. David and Alex were over by the Barneses' door, just staring.

"Psst! David!" Traci hissed at her brother in a loud whisper. She had to do it three times before he noticed and came over.

"What happened?" Traci asked.

"Alex's mom went into the kitchen, then she started screaming like she was being killed. She came hopping and spinning and screaming into the living room and out the door. Mr. Barnes chased her. Do you know what's the matter with her?"

Just then Lisa came tearing out of her house. "Dad! Dad!" she was yelling. "Grasshoppers! Gross giant grasshoppers! One hopped out of the kitchen right at me," and she started to cry.

"Is it just locusts?" asked David. "These people are going crazy about locusts?"

"Kids," it was Daddy, "I want you to get into the Barneses' house and catch the locusts." Then he frowned. "And I'd sure like to know how they got there."

Lisa and Mrs. Barnes stayed outside while the rest of

37

us got the locusts out of the house. David had worked hard collecting them. There must have been about twenty of them. They were in the curtains, on the counter, everywhere. Some had even gotten down the hall into the bedrooms.

The trouble was, Daddy was catching locusts, too, and he already looked tired.

About halfway through, David was taking one out the back door when he found his locust cage. He came charging inside, waving it around in the air and yelling about a thief. There were still a couple of locusts in it, too. Suddenly he marched straight up to Alex and swung at him.

"I didn't touch your dumb cage," yelled Alex, hopping backwards and trying to fend David off. Daddy strode over and grabbed both boys by a shoulder.

"Is this your doing, David?" he demanded. Sick or not, he looked pretty fierce. I was glad he wasn't asking me that question.

"No way," David was so mad his voice came out high and squeaky.

Traci and Sandy were already out in the yard, and I had just about made it through the door, but it didn't do any good. Daddy followed me out.

"Stop right there! Did you girls have anything to do with this?" he said very quietly and severely.

None of us was in a hurry to answer, but before we even got a chance Lisa burst out, "I hate this place. Everyone here is terrible!" She pointed straight at me. "She tried to stick some kind of ugly lizard on me, then she shoved some other gross bug right in Dad's face. Now the house is full of monster grasshoppers. I bet she did that, too."

"Lisa, take it easy. Maybe it was just a practical joke," said Mr. Barnes, walking over to her.

She swung around to face him. "I hate your dumb old practical jokes, too. I want to go home."

"This is our home now. We're here to serve God, and I think you could pull a little more of your own weight. Now get to your room."

"I can't! It's full of bugs, thanks to her," and she pointed at me again. "I bet God hates me, too!" With that, she marched off into the night.

There was a long silence. Finally Daddy said, "Let's get the rest of the locusts out of the house first. We can get to the root of this later. I'm very sorry about this, Joey."

I didn't like the sound of getting "to the root of this later." It wasn't fair. Lisa had blamed everything on me.

Mr. Barnes kept acting jolly and saying it was only a practical joke and that Lisa had better grow up.

A few minutes later Traci and I ended up in Alex's bedroom chasing one of the last locusts. "Why did you have to go and leave David's cage here?" I hissed at her in a whisper.

"Shhhh," she hissed back just as Alex walked in.

I grabbed at the locust. It hopped straight at Alex. He grabbed and caught it, but he dropped it in a hurry.

"Ow!" he yelled, shaking his poked hand. Locusts have little spines on the back of their hoppers. They can kick hard enough to poke them right into you. You have to grab their back legs so they can't kick you.

Alex looked so funny hopping around sucking his poked hand that Traci and I both laughed. He grabbed the locust again, only this time he got it the right way and ran at us. I just barely escaped having the thing stuffed down my back. He was grinning like a mad rat when we ran out of his room.

By the time we were done, my hands were poked sore, and I was sick of looking at the locusts' little legs and bulgy eyes. The grilling Sandy and I got when we were back at the house wasn't much of an improvement on locust chasing, though. David didn't come with us, so I guess Mom had said he could sleep at the Barneses' house.

"Traci, you go to your room," Daddy said as soon as we came in the house. She was already all set up in the guest room. She was sleeping there because Mom said she wanted us to sleep and not giggle all night.

As soon as Traci was gone Daddy started in. "The Barneses are having a rough time adjusting right now, and you girls have made it more difficult for them. I expected better things of both of you. Especially you, Anika. You're old enough to know better. Joey Barnes has a lot to offer to the Bible school, as does Elsie."

"But Daddy, I don't see why they have to wreck our trip to the coast," said Sandy.

"Whether they wreck it for you or not is entirely up to you. I don't always find Joey Barnes easy to get along with, but he has a real heart for God. He'll adapt, and maybe we can learn something from him."

"Like how to put rocks in hubcaps?" I asked. I could hardly bear the thought of Daddy having to work at getting along with Mr. Barnes.

"That's enough! Do you want to send someone away whom God has sent here?"

"What does that have to do with it?" I demanded.

Mom answered. "Elsie Barnes mentioned that if Lisa hasn't settled in here in the next several months, they would think seriously of going back to the States."

All I could say was, "Oh." I really hadn't thought that anything I did could make a difference, other than maybe stopping the Barneses from coming to the coast. And I still thought that was the right thing to do. I mean, God wanted Daddy to get better, didn't he? I was only helping. Helping something good to happen couldn't be wrong, could it? I didn't want to think about it, especially since I was getting a stronger feeling all the time that bugging the Barneses was wrong.

Daddy just shook his head, looking at me. "You've got to think first, Anika, before you start some crazy plan," he said.

But Lisa was such a twit! And she and her fancy American clothes made me look like a total geek. Besides, she'd gone and blamed everything on me when I didn't catch the ani-ngongo or put the locusts in their house or anything.

I got madder and madder thinking about it, and soon it seemed like it was all Lisa's fault. If she hadn't been acting so dumb her parents wouldn't be thinking of going back. Besides, if she and her mom weren't such scaredy cats *none* of this would have happened. They just weren't cut out to be missionaries, as far as I was concerned.

I didn't really listen to the rest of the lecture, but I knew it was over because Mom called Traci back for family devotions. They seemed to take forever, and I didn't feel like praying at all.

The next day was terrible. After breakfast Sandy and I had to go down to apologize to the Barneses. As soon as we got out of the house we started fighting. Sandy said

the ani-ngongo and the locusts had been my idea, and
now I'd gotten her in trouble, too. I said it was her idea
to start the whole bugging the Barneses thing in the
first place and told her to shut up. Then at the Barneses
she wouldn't say anything, so I had to do all the apolo-
gizing.

"I'm sorry about the locusts, Mrs. Barnes," I said.
"We didn't mean to make it harder for you." That was
true anyway.

"I'm sure you sweeties didn't mean any harm with
your little jokes. We just aren't used to everything here
quite yet," she gushed. "Now, Lisa, tell these nice girls
that you accept their apology."

Lisa just glared at us. She probably noticed that I
hadn't apologized to her. Well, she hadn't apologized
for blaming everything on me, either.

We stood there waiting for Lisa to say something for
at least two days. Well, that's how long it felt, anyway.
Finally Mrs. Barnes sent her to her room. I could tell
Lisa thought *that* was my fault, too.

Just as we were leaving, Mrs. Barnes said, "Girls,
we'll be spending so much time together at the coast,
you can't go on calling me Mrs. Barnes. I'm your very
own Aunt Elsie now."

That's what you think, I thought angrily. Then it
sunk in: they were coming to the coast with us. That

didn't exactly improve my day. When I told Mom and Dad, though, they were glad.

"Elsie Barnes is a brave woman," Mom said.

I spent the rest of the day reading. Reading is great when you don't want to think about anything that's happening in real life. Too bad it didn't really help this time. Mom kept getting after me to help with the packing. Then Daddy got really mad when I didn't come right away when he called me. I only wanted to finish the chapter I was reading. Finally, Mom gave me a lecture on "choosing to be miserable." This definitely was turning into a first-class, royally rotten day!

Usually I'm happy and excited before we go to the coast, but this time was the pits. Daddy let Mom talk him out of packing the car, which was always his job. He must have been feeling rotten. It made me ache inside to watch him. He ended up doing quite a bit of the work anyway, because we couldn't seem to get it just right.

When we went up to bed, Traci and Sandy begged and begged to share a room, but Mom wouldn't budge. After we were in bed, Sandy told me that Traci was really mad at David for showing the cage and getting everybody in trouble.

"Then she shouldn't have left it there. Traci always blames everything on other people," I snapped. "Just like you," I ended, which wasn't really fair.

"I do n—," Sandy started to say, but I interrupted.

"Shhh! Listen." There was a horrible noise outside, and it was coming closer. It was a man screaming. Then he was on the porch hammering on the door, sobbing and hollering, *"Saidia mimi! Saidia mimi!"* which means "Help me" in Swahili.

I shot out of bed, and Sandy was right behind me. In the sewing room next to our room, there is this sort of closet space you can get into. At the back you can see down through a screen onto the porch. We crawled into that closet and stared down. A second later Traci crawled in beside us.

Daddy was holding a flashlight for Mom, who was trying to see into the man's ear. The man kept on moaning something about bugs. Finally they put him in the car, and Mom drove off with him.

Dad came upstairs. I guess he knew we'd be up. He said that the man had been sleeping when an orange beetle had crawled into his ear. Beetles can be really strong, and this one kept clawing around in there.

"His ear was bleeding so badly your Mother couldn't see properly," said Daddy. "She's taken him into Machakos to the hospital."

If Daddy hadn't been sick, he would have been the one to drive the man to the hospital. I hated all the changes that Daddy's hepatitis was making. I glanced at

Sandy to see how she reacted to all this, but it seemed she didn't even notice or care.

After Daddy left, I lay in bed thinking about it. I prayed for Daddy, but it felt all wrong. Instead of feeling better, I just felt squirmy about what we'd been doing to the Barneses—so I quit praying. Finally I sat up in bed to look at Sandy. If anybody should care, Sandy should. I mean, she's a pain sometimes, but Daddy is her dad, too.

"Sandy?" I whispered. The hump in her bed never budged.

I bet she's faking, I thought, growing angry. *Fine! So ignore me then.* I'd wanted to talk to her about Daddy and apologize for arguing and stuff, but no way was I going to do that now. I lay down and stared at the ceiling. My eyes felt scratchy and my throat hurt, and I was sure I'd never get to sleep.

I did though. I never even heard Mom come back. You always have to wait for ages at hospitals in Kenya because they're so crowded with people who need help.

"Anika, Sandy, time to get moving!" Daddy was calling us. Sandy didn't even budge. She still hadn't moved by the time I was dressed, so I shook her bed hard.

"Come on, Daddy called us. Get up."

She was just kind of sitting up when I went downstairs. Mom and Dad didn't say anything about Sandy, even when she was late for breakfast. We usually get in trouble for that. Finally Traci went up to get her.

"Mom, what happened to the man who came in the night?" I asked, taking a big bite of toast.

"He's OK now. A doctor poured oil in his ear to drown the beetle and finally got it out with some long forceps. The man will have a sore ear for a while, though." She rubbed the back of her neck wearily. "I must admit I'm moving slowly this morning, too. I didn't get back from the hospital until around one in the morning." She sighed. "Well, let's get moving. We don't want the Barneses to have to wait for us."

The trunks of food and towels, snorkeling gear, dishes, and all the stuff that goes with a trip to the coast were already in the car. We just had to clean up breakfast, make the picnic lunch, and put rugs on the car seats. The rugs kept us from sticking to the car seats and getting all sweaty when it gets hot. But even with rugs, I wasn't looking forward to sharing the back seat with Traci and Sandy. Fortunately, David was riding with the Barneses.

"I bet we'll have to wait for hours for the Barneses to be ready," I muttered as I stuck a couple of books up behind the seat to read on the way.

Sandy had finally finished breakfast and was tucking

the rugs over the seats. "Probably," she said. "I hate it when we have to wait ages for somebody."

"The way Mrs. Barnes talks so slow, she's probably still halfway through calling Alex and David to wake up," said Traci.

Mom and Daddy came out, and, like always, we prayed about the trip before we even started the car. Mom and Daddy prayed for the Barneses, and especially for Lisa. I just prayed that Daddy would rest and get better.

One thing was good: we were wrong about the Barneses being late. They were just getting into the car when we drove over. Daddy waved them on ahead, and we were off.

Sandy and Traci started playing hangman. I watched the people along the road. There were ladies on their way to market carrying big baskets of vegetables on their backs. There were kids walking to school in their uniforms—khaki shorts and tops for the boys and dusty blue dresses for the girls. There were lots of men going to work on their big black bicycles. One man was carrying a mattress on his bike; another had tied a whole basket of chickens onto his bike.

Sandy and I usually compete to see who can spot the first wild animals when we get out of the Machakos hills into the grasslands, but she'd gone to sleep halfway through the hangman game. I wondered if she was sick. Mom wouldn't let Traci wake her up.

I saw a herd of Tommies, little gazelles that look kind of like tiny deer. And a herd of giraffe that lives out by Button's Pimple was right by the road.

Daddy was busy dodging the big potholes in the road. Every now and then he'd dodge one on our side and come real close to a lorry—an old diesel truck that stinks like mad and goes very slowly—coming the other way. Whenever he did that, Mom yelled, "Keeviin!"

We were out of the grassland and into the hotter grey thorn brush when the Barneses' car swerved right across the road.

"Watch out!" Mom yelled as their car spun right toward us. Daddy slammed on the brakes so hard Sandy banged her face on the back of his seat. The Barneses missed us and ended up backward in the ditch.

"Look at their tire!" I said as soon as we stopped. There were chunks of tire all over. Their wheel rim had left a big gouge across the dirt on the side of the road.

Daddy jumped out and ran over to their car. I'd just gotten my door open when Mom said, "You girls stay put until we know what's happening."

That's when Traci noticed Sandy's bloody nose.

Mom sent me to get the thermos of cold water out of

the trunk. It wasn't until Sandy was lying on the back-seat while Mom held a big blob of cold, wet Kleenex on her nose that Mom finally let me go over to see what was happening. Traci followed me.

By then Daddy and Mr. Barnes were changing the tire.

Mr. Barnes looked up at us, "How did you like my stunt driving?" he said and started laughing. "Wheew, I wouldn't want to do that too often."

He made a big act out of wiping his forehead. There was a chorus of high-pitched giggles. Mr. Barnes looked so surprised that I guessed he hadn't noticed that we were surrounded by a ring of African kids. That happens whenever you break down near African farms.

Most of us were used to having an audience. Traci didn't care—she just looked at the tire and headed back to our car to be with Sandy. Alex didn't seem to mind, either. He and David were running around picking up chunks of tire. But Lisa and Mrs. Barnes were edged up close to the car, looking nervous. Suddenly Mrs. Barnes shook her head and stepped away from the car toward the African kids. I guessed she'd decided to try out her Swahili on them.

She said, *"Jambo,"* which means hello, only she said it like "Jayam bow," which isn't how you say it. The kids made a noise like "Aieeeee," and giggled behind their hands. One of the bigger boys decided to try out his English. He stuck out his hand and said, "Give me a sweet."

Mrs. Barnes looked at me and said, "What does he want?"

"Candy, but don't give him any."

"Whyever not?" she asked and went straight to the car and got out a bag of peppermints.

As soon as the kids saw what she had, she was mobbed. They crowded up around her, yelling and reaching out their hands. More kids came running from every direction, their bare feet kicking up the red dust. She passed out candy like mad, but she was getting pushed back toward the car.

Daddy looked up at the noise, stood up, and said, *"Hapana!"*—"no" in Swahili—very loudly. He had to do it twice before the kids looked at him. Then he told them that they should know better and to go home. They just grinned and backed off, but still stayed to watch.

"I see what you mean now, honey," Mrs. Barnes said to me. "My, but those children are simply filthy."

"It's hard to stay clean when all the water your family uses has to be carried for miles from a river or a well that isn't too clean itself," said Daddy.

"Well, we certainly can't eat what's left of this bag of candy. It's too dirty now."

"Here," I said. She gave it to me. I took it over and gave it to one of the bigger boys. He took off running with most of the other kids after him.

When all the kids had first approached us, Lisa had gone to stand close to Mr. Barnes. She was still practically on top of him.

"Lisa, back off. I can't see what I'm doing," said Mr. Barnes.

"Why don't you and Anika go sit in our car?" asked Daddy.

Lisa just glared at me. I could tell she wasn't about to go anywhere with me, and I felt the same about her. Neither of us budged.

To change the subject, I asked, "How can people grow enough food to eat here, Daddy? It's so dry."

"They often don't," Daddy said. "Africa has such a terrible problem with overpopulation that many of these people have moved here in the last fifteen years because there is no space for them elsewhere." He didn't say anything more about me going to sit in the car with Lisa.

When we finally got going again, Daddy actually let Mom drive. He never lets Mom drive, so I figured he was feeling even worse than usual. Sandy's nose had stopped bleeding, but she still looked really wiped out. What was wrong with her?

Daddy said he wasn't surprised Mr. Barnes had blown a tire, because he'd noticed they weren't dodging a lot of the potholes. "He's just lucky he didn't wreck the rim of the tire. It looked OK to me." After Daddy said that he paused for a second, then added, "I guess it's not just luck. God is looking after all of us. We could easily have hit them."

"Let's thank him," Mom said. So we did.

After we prayed, Daddy said, "I sure hope we can find a tire at Hunter's Lodge."

"Can't the Barneses just keep going with the tires that are on there now?" I asked.

"Driving on this road with no spare tire would be absolute lunacy, especially the way Joey's been hitting the potholes."

"Well, tell him not to," Sandy said.

"Everybody has to learn to adjust to a new place in their own way," Mom said. It was no use arguing. I flopped back in my seat, crossing my arms with an angry sigh.

Already the Barneses were wrecking our trip to the coast.

Chapter Four

There were absolutely no tires at Hunter's Lodge. The adults decided we should drive slowly and carefully down to Mtitondei, where there might be a tire.

It was really hot now. We drove with the windows wide open. My hair whipped in the wind and bothered my eyes. We had shorts on, and Traci's sweaty legs kept bumping against mine and sticking.

"Move over," I snapped.

"I can't, there isn't room," she said.

I'd just started to say that there was, too, when Mom interrupted, "First one to see an elephant gets a Coke at Mtitondei."

Traci and Sandy quit bugging me and started looking out the window. I looked, too. A cold Coke sounded super right then. We were going really slowly so the Barneses wouldn't get another flat, so it was easy to look.

"There!" Traci yelled, practically in my ear. She was right. You could just see a rusty red back behind some thorn trees. Mom slowed the car down, and we all leaned out the windows and pointed so that the Barneses would see it, too. They never did, though. I guess they didn't expect red elephants. Not that the animals are really red. They just look rusty red because they like to take dirt baths, and the dirt around that area is red.

Sandy asked, "Mom can we get some samosas and stuff at Mtitondei, please, please? I'm hungry already, and it's going to be forever until we have lunch at Tsavo River." Sandy and David both loved samosas, which are spicy little triangle-shaped meat pies. Some of them are so spicy hot that they can nearly blow your ears off.

"Please, Aunt Hazel, can we?" Traci chimed in.

"Well, OK," Mom said, "but make sure you don't leave Lisa out. I'll get you all pop, too. Just be sure you wipe off the top of the bottle before you open it."

She always says that. As if we didn't know that the dirt could give us amoebic dysentery, or even hepatitis like Dad had—especially at a place with so many people around. Actually, I didn't care as much as Mom wanted me to. Everybody got amoeba once in a while, but those of us who had lived in Kenya all our lives didn't usually get very sick. I figured it was adults and new people who really ought to watch out.

The Chyulu Hills were along the south of the road we were passing. The hills are made of lava and have the craziest shapes—they look like cast-iron whipped cream. They're dry and harsh and rough. I'd heard that people sometimes trek in to climb the cliffs there. I'd have loved to go do that.

At Mtitondei, everybody except Daddy and Mr. Barnes walked over to the duka—the shop—together. It was like most dukas, absolutely packed full of everything from thongs to boxes of English tea biscuits.

"Hey, you guys, watch Alex eat this," David called. He had talked Alex into buying a hot samosa.

"Come on Alex, go for it," David said.

Alex took a little nibble off the corner.

"Come on, take a *big* bite," said David.

Alex looked at him. "You eat yours first."

"Like this?" asked David, taking a huge bite. "See? It's great," he said with his mouth full. He wasn't letting on how hot it really was, but I noticed his forehead was sweating.

Lisa had been over with our moms, but she walked over just then and butted in. "Alex, don't. It's some sort of trick."

He looked straight at her and took a huge bite anyway. Then his eyes bugged out, but he didn't spit it out. Everybody giggled at the expression on his face.

He swallowed hard and yelled, "*Whooooo!*" grabbing David's pop and taking a big swig. Then he said, "Hey, give me one of those things. I'm going to get Dad."

"Aleeeex!" Lisa sounded really exasperated.

"OK, you eat it then, if you're so smart," he said.

She took it and, looking really disgusted, took a normal-sized bite. I could hardly wait for her reaction.

"Hey, this is good," she said and took another bite.

At first I thought she was faking. We really looked dumb, all staring at her waiting for her to go red in the face or something.

She put her chin in the air and said, "They're the only good thing in Kenya, as far as I'm concerned. And they're not even as good as enchiladas."

Yeah, well, she's welcome to enchiladas—whatever they are, I thought. If she'd even halfway try, she might like it here. I looked out at the horizon. Far, far off I could see Kilimanjaro, the tallest mountain in Africa. Its smooth snowy peak was sitting like a tiny white Frisbee just above the horizon. How could anybody hate such a beautiful place?

I walked over to get a Coke, and Sandy and Traci followed me. A couple of minutes later, Mrs. Barnes and Lisa came over.

"Girls, could you kindly tell us where we could find the facilities?" Mrs. Barnes asked.

It took me a second to figure out that she was looking for the toilet. I just grinned and didn't answer.

Sandy figured out what she meant a second later and
said, "It's over there on the side of the building. But it's
really gross."

As soon as they left, Traci, Sandy, and I started to giggle. The toilets at Mtitondei were one thing that would
definitely bug the Barneses. They were horrible. I kind
of needed to go, too, but there was no way I was going
to use the toilets there. Not unless I was totally desper-
ate! Usually, we just waited until we reached Tsavo
River and stopped for lunch. Even the bushes there
were better than the "facilities" at Mtitondei.

Some people finally left one of the sticky little tables
by the dukas, so Mom, Traci, Sandy, and I sat down.
The sun felt like warm syrup on my shoulders. I looked
around at all the different kinds of people. It was more
fun to watch them and try to guess who they were than
it was to listen to Sandy and Traci talk to Mom.

There was an East Indian family with about five kids
and two grandmas who were wearing saris—they probably owned a shop somewhere. Then there were some
German tourists, complete with cameras and sun-
burns. I couldn't decide if one very British lady with a
fat toddler was a settler's wife or not. But the best one
was a big blond man who was tanned almost black. He

wore baggy khaki shorts, looked terribly fierce, and sat at a table all by himself. He looked like he belonged in the kinds of adventures I only imagined.

It seemed like we waited there forever. Finally, though, the tire was fixed and we could leave. It's not very far from Mtitondei to Tsavo River. We usually stopped and ate our picnic lunch there because it's so nice by the river. There's no picnic site, though, just a dirt track that goes down by the river.

The yellow river pours over huge flat rocks in the bright sun. It comes out of the Tsavo hills. Tsavo is a national park, a place of dry thorn bushes, baobab trees, and wild animals. Poachers with machine guns had killed almost all the rhinos and lots of the elephants that used to live there.

Once we got there, I went to throw rocks in the river and think about the crocodiles. I'd never seen one there, but I liked to think about them. They were like a dangerous secret in the wild yellow river. Lisa and Mrs. Barnes refused to leave their car. They even ate in there.

After lunch, as we drove along, both Daddy and Sandy went to sleep. I looked at Sandy. She wasn't getting hepatitis, too, was she?

I sat in my corner of the backseat and worried about Sandy and Lisa and Daddy. I didn't cheer up until the air started to change. We were out of the national parks and out of the desert. There were people on the sides of the road again, only now they carried loads on their heads instead of on their backs. The air was humid. It smelled like rotten fruit, spices, seaweed, and ocean salt. We were almost there.

On the long curves into the city of Mombasa, we got stuck behind a lorry loaded with pineapples. Mr. Barnes was afraid to pass. Waves of stinky black smoke poured over the Barneses' car and back to us.

"Mom, let's just go past," I said. "This lorry stinks."

"Please, Aunt Hazel," Traci added. "We'll never get there going this slow. Please?"

"Shhhh! You'll wake Kevin and Sandy," Mom said. "We can't get ahead and leave Joey Barnes to get lost. We'll just have to be patient until he adjusts to Kenya."

I sighed and turned to look out the window. Lining the path beside the road were bulgy, bottle-shaped baobab trees, coconut palms that looked like skinny teenagers with wild hair, and dark green mango trees with thick trunks.

"The biggest mango trees were planted by Arab slave traders," Mom said.

"Why did they plant mango trees?" Traci demanded. "I don't think I want to eat mangoes anymore."

"The mangoes helped to feed the slaves," Mom said. "That was more than a hundred years ago. There were no roads then, only paths. As far as eating mangoes is concerned, I wouldn't worry about it. Just because someone has used one of God's good gifts wrongly doesn't mean it can't be used properly. I muv langoes."

Traci and I laughed, and Mom looked frustrated. I went back to looking out the window. It was creepy thinking of lines of slaves being driven where the road was now.

It was dark by the time we turned off on the bumpy little dirt road to Bilge Water. We were halfway down it when we realized Mr. Barnes wasn't behind us. Dad was awake by now—and looking worried. *I knew those Barneses were going to keep Daddy from resting,* I thought angrily.

"Kevin, let me drop you off first. You're really tired," Mom said. "I can go back and look for them."

"No, that would just waste time," Daddy said. "They can't be far. They turned off right behind us. I'll drive now."

"Daddy, let Mom drop us off with you. Please?" I interrupted.

"Yes, Daddy, please? Please? Let Mom look for them," said Sandy. Traci just kept her mouth shut. I guess she didn't want to get in on a family fight.

He just ignored us. A few minutes later we were bumping back down the way we came. Daddy was wrong about finding them in a hurry. We went all the way back to the main road without finding them. I was getting madder and madder all the time.

"Where on earth bould they kee," Mom said. She's always worse when she's worried.

Daddy laughed and answered, "Baybe they tould have curned off on a side road."

"Daddeeeee!" yelled Sandy, "Don't! How can you make jokes when you're probably dying, and you don't even care, and you wouldn't let Mom find the stupid Barneses so you can rest," and she burst out crying.

I just sat there with my mouth open. Sandy *did* care about Daddy.

"Sandy, settle down," Mom broke in. "You know perfectly well your father isn't dying. We talked about that last night. You're just overtired."

I demanded to know when Mom had talked to Sandy.

"Sandy was awake worrying about your father when I got back from taking the man to the hospital," Mom answered. "Now both of you just simmer down and help us look for the Barneses."

So that's what was wrong with Sandy. She and Mom had been up talking half the night, when all the time I thought she couldn't care beans about Daddy. So why didn't she answer me when I called her, if she wasn't asleep?

Daddy never even said anything. We pulled in at a duka where some African men were sitting drinking beer around a lantern and asked if they'd seen the Barneses' car. They pointed down another road. After that it only took a few minutes to find them. They'd fallen behind and taken a wrong turn.

At Bilge Water I didn't even ask if we could run down to the beach first like we usually did. Sandy and I started to unpack the car like mad. I guess we both had the same idea: the more we did, the less Daddy could do.

Traci was just kind of standing around watching.

"Come on, Traci, help!" Sandy said, sounding irritated.

"Mom and Dad always let us go down to the beach first," Traci answered, but she did pick up a sleeping bag and kind of wandered into the house with it.

Daddy was still untying the stuff on top. I tried to drag the trunk full of food into the kitchen, which is separate from the house.

"Anika, use your head," Daddy snapped. "That's way too heavy for you. Joey Barnes and I will get it later." He must have been really tired, because he's not usually so crabby.

I took the cots in. Mom was kind of directing, so I asked her where to put them.

"In the room all you girls will share," she answered.

"*All* the girls?" I asked, just to make sure I'd heard right.

"You, Sandy, Traci, and Lisa will be sharing that room," she said very slowly and clearly. (You know how parents sound when they're really irritated.)

Oh joy, I thought. *I get to share a room with Lisa Barnes.*

Sandy was already in the room putting down a load of sleeping bags.

"I wanted to talk to you about Daddy last night, and you wouldn't even answer," I blurted. That wasn't what I'd meant to say, and it sounded bad. I tried again, "I mean, I thought you didn't even care about Daddy."

"How was I supposed to know that's what you wanted to talk about? I thought *you* didn't care till Mom said you were worried, too. You never even talked about it or anything."

"Neither did you! Why did you think I was trying to keep the Barneses from coming to the coast?"

"I thought you just didn't like Lisa and didn't want to share," she said.

Just then Lisa walked in. We shut up. I didn't know if she'd heard what we said or not. Anyway, she totally ignored us, put down her suitcase, and walked out.

"Do you like her, then?" I asked, kind of sarcastically.

Sandy just rolled her eyes.

"At least they don't expect you to be her best friend," I said. "Come on, let's get the car unloaded."

When we were done unpacking, everybody went down to the beach together. Mom tried to talk Daddy into resting, but he said the walk would help him relax. It was dark out, which made it hard to see the sandy footpath, but I ran ahead anyway. Red dirt crumbled under my feet as I felt my way through the little gully where the path cut through the dirt cliff above the beach. Then I was there.

The white sand gleamed, even in starlight. The ocean roared far off against the outer reef. I glanced out and saw it was low tide. I stepped out of my thongs and ran across the cool, silver sand. An army of tiny ghosts fled in front of my feet, and I knew they were beach crabs. The air stroked my hot, sticky skin, and I did a cart-wheel just because it was so great to be there.

Voices came down from the path, and little circles of gold light from the flashlight danced all around. I walked away from them, down across the wet, ridged sand below the high tide mark, and stopped when my feet touched cool, salty water. The black, velvet sky was packed full of stars, and I felt like I could hear them sing if only everybody else would be still. The world was a wide open beautiful space, full of God's glory.

"God, please let Daddy get better," I whispered. I felt really uneasy inside and thought about Lisa. I looked far out where the breakers roared and shone white. I'd had to memorize Proverbs 3:5-6, and it came into my head right then: "Trust the Lord completely; don't ever trust yourself. In everything you do, put God first, and he will direct you and crown your efforts with success."

It was really obvious all of a sudden that I'd been "trusting myself." I'd been trying to make things turn out the way I thought they should by getting the Barneses not to come to the coast. Suddenly I knew God didn't want me to be mean to the Barneses, no matter what—and I felt terrible.

"I'm sorry, God," I whispered. "I'll try to trust you. I'll even try to be nice to Lisa Barnes. Only please let Daddy get better. Please don't let us have to go back to the States."

I could just feel God's love all around me in the wide open starry night. Mom and Daddy and the others were coming toward me across the sand, but I didn't feel like being around anybody, so I took off down the beach.

At Bilge Water the beach is in little coves with big jags of old black coral separating one piece of beach from the next. Without really thinking, I started going across the smoother coral below the tide mark to get to the next beach. *Splash!* My foot slipped, and I sat down hard in a tide pool. I didn't land on any sea urchins, but it still hurt.

"Anika, was that you? Are you OK?" It was Mom.

"Yes," I called back. I didn't want anybody to see how dumb I'd been. Walking by tide pools in the dark is not smart. Suddenly, I wondered what else was in the tide pool with me. I mean, I love tide pools. All kinds of neat creatures live there, but they don't much appreciate someone sitting on them. Some of them have pretty powerful ways of disapproving. I'd missed the sea urchin's spines, but what about sting-rays or scorpion fish?

I started to move, but stopped. "Think for once," I muttered to myself. I could have shifted my behind right onto a sea urchin.

"Mom, could you bring a flashlight?" I asked. They probably were going to lecture me on not using my head, but I'm used to that—and it would sure beat being stabbed by sea urchin spines . . . or worse.

Of course, everybody had to come over at once. Sandy got there first, and shone the flashlight straight into my eyes. I felt incredibly dumb sitting in the water, blinking at the light.

I covered my eyes. "Sandy! Shine it in the water. I want to see where there aren't any sea urchins so I can get out."

I was just climbing out when Mom got there.

"Are you sure you're OK, Anika?" she asked, looking at me carefully. "Whatever possessed you to walk over here in the dark?"

"You could have stepped on a stone fish and died," said Traci, sounding pleased.

"Wow, look at all the sea urchins," David said and grabbed the flashlight to shine it around at the water. The whole area was covered in sea urchins.

"Well, if you managed not to get any spines in you, your guardian angel was sure on duty tonight," Daddy said.

"Neat," said Alex, and reached for an urchin. A couple of people started to yell, but it was too late. He jerked his hand back, but he'd already been poked. Luckily the spines hadn't broken off in his hand.

You could tell he wanted to cry. Sea urchin spines really hurt. He didn't cry, though. He just stood there sucking his finger. I felt sorry for him.

"Here, I'll show you," I said. "You just have to be real careful, and get ahold of one spine to pick them up."

I picked up an urchin that was sitting in the flash-light beam, then set it very gently on my palm. Sea urchins come in different styles. Some have three-inch-long, tiger-striped spines, or short, pale purple spines. But this one was an ordinary black one. It walked across my palm with its spines and dropped back into the water.

"Anika, that's enough of that," said Daddy. "Let's get back onto the sand before someone else gets spines in them."

We were all back on the sand when Alex joined us, triumphantly carrying a sea urchin on his palm. I couldn't figure out how he'd been able to see the urchin without the flashlight shining right on it.

"Gross! Mom, make him put it back," Lisa screeched.

He did, too, which was actually good. It would just die and stink if he took it up to the house.

Back at the house, I had to take a shower to get the salt off from when I'd fallen in the tide pool. When I got back to the room, it looked peaceful. Sandy and Traci had stuck their cots next to each other and were talking. Lisa was sitting on one of the regular beds opening her suitcase.

Lisa suddenly said, "Yuk!" and put her hands over her face.

"What's the matter?" I asked. After all, I had promised God I'd be nice to Lisa.

She never even answered, so I walked over to see. Lisa's pajamas were stiff with gooey green stuff. It took me a second to realize it was shampoo. Mom always made us put our shampoo bottles in plastic bags, but

Lisa hadn't done that with hers and the top had come off.

She turned her back on me. I could tell she was crying.

"Lisa, it's OK," I said. "Do you want me to get your mom?"

"No!" She practically yelled it.

"OK, OK, I won't." I paused a second to think. "I know, I'll lend you some pj's, and Ali can get the shampoo out of your clothes tomorrow."

Ali was the worker who took care of Bilge Water for the owners. He was mostly a fisherman, but he cut the grass when he felt like it and cleaned the house after somebody was there. We paid him extra to do clothes and dishes.

Still facing the wall, Lisa said very fiercely, "No! Even if I am stuck here, nobody's going to make me be a slave driver."

"What are you talking about?" I was really puzzled. "Nobody said anything about slaves."

"You all think you're so great, being missionaries, but you make the Africans work for you like slaves. I hate it here!" and she started really crying.

Up until now, Traci and Sandy had been ignoring Lisa completely, but that was too much for Traci.

Traci interrupted, "I suppose you think not having a worker makes you better?" Her voice sounded really mad. "You're so smart with your cool clothes from California that you think you're too good to have a worker. Well, I hope you know that because of you, Mbaika has no job and no money to send her kids to school. I hope that makes you feel really righteous."

Traci really liked Mbaika. She used to be the Stewarts' worker. When they went on furlough, though, Mbaika started working for another family. So when the Stewarts got back, they'd gotten a new worker. Traci used to visit with Mbaika a lot. Then the other family had retired, and the Barneses had gotten their house. I never even thought about whom Mbaika would work for. I guess Traci thought Mbaika would work for the Barneses.

"Oh, come on, Traci," I interrupted. "She probably doesn't even know who Mbaika is."

"Well, she shouldn't spend all her time crying in her room, then," said Traci.

"Leave her alone," I said. "Here Lisa, I'll help you sort out the stuff with shampoo on it."

Lisa was still facing the wall and crying, only not so loud now. When she didn't budge, I started sorting through her stuff. She had the cutest clothes. Anyway, I took the dirty clothes to Mom and put my spare pj's on Lisa's bed. Lisa still wouldn't turn around. I finally went to bed.

Chapter
Five

The next morning I woke up just as it was starting to get light out. I knew that the edge of the ocean early in the morning is the finest place in the world. It's best if you're alone, so I put my clothes on quietly and snuck out. All I saw of Lisa was the top of her head sticking out of her sleeping bag.

It was a cool, quiet, secret morning. There were still stars showing, but out on the edge of the sky—over the ocean—there was a pink and gold glow. All the colors of the reefs and tide pools were silvery.

Twice a day the water is deeper at the ocean. That's called high tide. That morning, the tide was on the way out. Already I could hear the breakers roaring far off against the outer reef. Near the beach the water lay still and quiet, reflecting the sky like a huge magic mirror.

I walked across the packed, cool sand and stepped carefully into the water. The ocean water made a tickly line, like a bracelet, around my ankles.

This water touches India, I thought and waded

deeper very slowly so I wouldn't ripple the surface. Salt water lapped the back of my knee, and the sand felt rough under my feet. Gold light and warmth washed over my body, and I looked up. The sun had painted a glittering gold road from the edge of the world to me.

Then I noticed a shape in the sun road. I squinted and looked again. A fisherman was poling his dugout canoe back to the beach. He looked like a black cutout against the bright water.

"Jambo," I called as he got close to the beach.

"Jambo, memsahib," he called back.

I ran toward him through the shallow water, making the glittering splashes go as high as I could. It was fun to see what fishermen had caught.

In the bottom of his canoe were two big stingrays. They looked like grey leather saddle pads with eyes. He also had some parrot fish strung on a string, like a bunch of neon-colored slimy beads.

"Do you want to buy fish?" he asked me in Swahili.

I said I didn't, but maybe my mother would. Parrot fish are really good to eat. *Maybe Ali will cook us samaki masala,* I thought, licking my lips. That's practically the best food there is: spicy deep-fried fish chunks.

"Where is your house?" he asked.

After I'd told him, I headed off down the beach. How

could I ever go back to the States and leave all this? Daddy just *had* to get better. I prayed for Daddy and then for Lisa. God was all around me in the shining morning, and his love made me feel brave.

When I got back for breakfast, Lisa wasn't there. I walked in just in time to hear Mrs. Barnes ask in a squeaky, worried voice, "Where could that girl have gotten to?"

"I wouldn't worry too much. She's probably just gone on a walk like Anika often does," Mom said. "Oh, here's Anika now."

"Anika, did you see Lisa on the beach?" Daddy asked.

I said, "No." Mrs. Barnes looked even more worried, so I added, "She probably just went the other way."

"Well, if you all'd be so kind as to tell us which way you went, Joey and I'll go the other way and look for her," she drawled. "But you just sit down and eat yourself a good breakfast first."

I said, "Yes, Mrs. Barnes," and started peeling a tiny, fat thumb banana. Its firm sweetness filled my mouth. *Mmm,* I thought, *you can only get really good ones at the coast.*

Mrs. Barnes came around the table and patted my back, "Now, now, don't you go Mrs. Barnesing me. I'm your very own Aunt Elsie, and don't you forget it."

I felt like squirming, but I managed not to.

"Did Lisa say anything to you girls about where she was going?" Daddy asked.

"She didn't say anything to us at all except that she thought we were slave drivers," Traci said. I could tell she was still mad from last night.

"Now that's too bad. You'll have to be patient with Lisa until she gets adjusted," boomed Mr. Barnes.

"She said you think it's wrong to have workers. Is that true?" I blurted, then wished I hadn't. I mean, it wasn't very polite.

Traci joined in and made it seem even ruder, "How about Mbaika? What's she supposed to do? Wait to eat till you get adjusted?"

"Ha, ha, ha!" Mr. Barnes boomed. "Think you've got me cornered do you? Well, I don't know who this Mbakila, or whatever, is, but we do think that we should do our own dirty work."

"Well, Mbaika used to be the Langs' worker," said Traci. She was going to tell him who Mbaika was whether he wanted to know or not. "She was going to work for you when they left, only you wouldn't hire her. Now she doesn't have any money to send her kids to school or anything." Traci flipped her hair back and glared at him.

"Why haven't we heard about this before?" Mr. Barnes asked, looking at Daddy.

"Well, Mbaika did come to you and ask for the job,"

he said. "We thought we should leave the choice up to you. No man should do what is against his conscience."

"Honey, we can talk about this another time," said Mrs. Barnes. "Right now we had better get looking for our daughter."

I got up to go with them and Daddy said, "I want you to come right back as soon as you've shown them which way you went. You, Sandy, Mom, and I have to have a talk."

I figured it must be about something important. Daddy doesn't call family conferences very often. We usually just talk at family devotions and stuff. Then I had an awful thought: maybe it was bad news about Daddy's hepatitis or something.

When I got back, Traci was sitting out front reading. "They're in your mom and dad's room, waiting for you," she said without even looking up.

Daddy made us all sit down on the bed.

"First of all, I'd like to say I'm sorry," he said. "I've been thinking a lot about what you said last night, Sandy, and I've decided you're right."

"What did she say?" I whispered to Mom.

Sandy heard me. "I guess he means what I said in the car. Right, Daddy?"

"Yes. Sandy said I was being selfish by refusing to stop working. At least, that's how I took it—"

"Oh, Daddy," she interrupted, "I was just upset."

"But you were right," he answered. "I'd been thinking that my main responsibility is to do God's work. Last night I realized my family is God's work, too. I mean, I knew that. Your mother and I have talked about it many times. But I guess it never really sank in before."

It felt strange hearing Daddy talk like that, so I ducked my head. Some of the stitches were coming out of the quilt on Mom and Dad's bed. I tried to get my fingernail under one. Daddy kept talking.

"God's given me the job of being husband and father, and to do that job I need to stay alive. I can't completely exhaust myself for mission work. So I want you to know that I'll be trying to discipline myself to rest. That's not easy for me, so I'd appreciate your prayers."

There was a little silence, then Mom said, "Let's pray together about it." And we did.

Now that I was through with bugging the Barneses, it was nice not to feel bad when I tried to pray. I even prayed for Lisa. But mostly we all prayed for Daddy to get better and rest.

With all of us praying, what else can he do? I thought. I forgot that God sometimes answers no to our prayers. Anyway, all of us were smiling when we finished praying. Then I remembered how worried Mr. and Mrs. Barnes were.

"How come Mr. Barnes is so worried about Lisa? Should we look for her or something?" I asked.

"Well, I'm not worried yet," Daddy answered. "She has probably just gone on a walk. It will just make things worse for her if we all get ourselves into a stew. Let's give her a little time."

"And let's do all we can to make her feel welcome here," said Mom, looking at me really hard.

I almost told her what I'd decided last night, but just then Alex and David came tearing into the house.

"Uncle Kevin, Uncle Kevin," David yelled as they ran in the door, "Ali said we could go with him octopus hunting. Can we? Can we?"

"Please?" added Alex.

That sounded interesting. I guess Sandy thought so, too, because she said, "Can Traci and I go, too?"

Daddy said, "If you want to have Ali come and talk to me about it, we'll see. I'll be out front in the shade resting."

It was sort of funny how he announced he'd be resting. I couldn't remember him ever doing that before. I smiled.

The sun was so bright when I went out that it made everything look all bleached out for a second. David and Alex ran off to get Ali, and he came lumbering around the house to talk to Daddy. Ali must have been part Arab, because he had sort of taffy-colored skin and curly hair on his chest. He looked solid and strong and sort of fat. He always wore a cloth around his middle that looked like a narrow-striped wrap-around skirt. It was called a *kikoi,* and many of the Africans at the coast wear them.

"*Jambo, Bwana,*" he said.

"*Jambo, Ali. Habari ya usiku leo?*" Daddy answered.

When they'd finally finished saying "Hello, How is the day? How is your family?" and so on (you always have to be superpolite in Swahili), they got down to the octopus hunting. Ali said we could come.

"When will you be returning?" Daddy asked.

Ali said the tide would be full out at ten so he would be back "at the fifth hour." That meant eleven o'clock, since the Swahilis count the hours of the day from when the sun comes up—which makes seven in the morning one o'clock. Actually, that has always made more sense to me than starting at midnight, like we do.

Daddy said we could go, so I took off looking for my reefing shoes, a stick, and some sunscreen.

Traci didn't want to go, and she managed to talk Sandy into staying with her. So Alex, David, and I followed Ali down to the beach and out onto the reef.

Ali was in a hurry, so we didn't have time to poke around in the sandy, seaweedy tide pools close to shore.

Just like always, sand got into my old tennies and felt all scratchy around my ankles. I kept curling my toes up and swishing my feet around in the water to try to get the sand out. It was great to be going out on the reef again.

Ali had to wait for us on the way out to the main reef. Most places the water was above his knees, but it was up to Alex's and David's waists. You have to watch where you step, too, because it's not flat.

I saw one really nice little live coral bommie—a sort of six-foot-tall cauliflower of coral—and promised myself I'd come back to it and snorkel. There's always loads of fish around the bommies.

The main reef was a tan shelf of coral about a hundred feet wide and one hundred miles long. When we got there, Ali started walking very slowly and peering into the tide pools on the inside edge. He looked like a fat heron, poking along and staring into the water.

He motioned us back, so I started poking around some other pools. The whole shelf of the reef is full of holes. Some are shallow, but others are five or six feet deep and almost that wide. All of them are full of creatures.

I squatted down beside one and held still. Everything is either hidden or looks like something other than what it really is, so you have to sit still and wait to see anything. The wind rumpled the water so it was hard to see in. Then the wind hushed.

After a second, a little seashell by the edge got up on tiny orange legs and fell into the pool. *That's just a hermit crab,* I thought. Then I focused on a lump on the coral side of the pool that didn't look quite right. I poked it gently with my stick, and it let loose. A little creature that looked like an oval saucer with bright blue and yellow stripes fluttered down across the pool. I didn't know what it really was—I called them sea butterflies.

"Hey, look at this!" It was Alex. He was holding up one of those black sea slugs. It started squirting out white stuff, and he dropped it.

"Alex, don't pick stuff up," I said standing up. The back of my knees felt cool all of a sudden. They'd gotten sweaty when I was squatting by the pool.

"Yes," said David. "Lots of stuff is poisonous."

"You're just trying to scare me," he said and grinned at us.

"Alex, I'm not, really," I said. On the reef, picking things up in your hand is idiotic. Besides, I didn't want to be blamed for him getting stung or whatever. "Ask Ali if you don't believe us."

"You'd just tell me he agreed with you no matter what he said," Alex answered still grinning. "I don't know Swahili, remember?"

"OK, then ask Daddy, but don't touch—"

A big splash from Ali's direction interrupted us. He was leaning over the edge of a pool with his arms in the water, and something was splashing like mad. We hopped across the rough coral toward him as quick as we could.

Long snaky tentacles ran up his arm. He slid his other hand down his wet muscular arm and pushed off the tentacles, which made a noise like ripping cloth. Then he grabbed the octopus with his other hand and made a strong twisting motion. It lay limp. Its skin was still changing colors in waves, but it was dead.

"How did you do that?" I asked, because I couldn't see how he'd killed it.

"He has no headbone," he said. "I turned his head out through his mouth."

Then he showed us two hard shiny brown bits that looked like a bird's beak and said, "This is dangerous. He can bite off your finger with this."

The octopus had tentacles as long as David was tall, but it looked like a pair of old wet pants dragging behind Ali in the water. It wasn't very big. Ali swished it clean and dumped it in the basket he was carrying.

When Ali started hunting again, I stayed closer. I wanted to know how he could tell an octopus was in a pool. I'd only seen one once when I was snorkeling with Daddy, and that was just luck.

I followed Ali quietly for a long time. My shoulders were baking hot from the sun, but I didn't stop to get wet like I usually did.

Ali suddenly pointed at the edge of a tide pool.

"Where?" I whispered.

"Just there. See?" He pointed with a metal stick he was carrying and put his basket down.

I stared and stared, but could not see anything that remotely resembled an octopus.

"Look," he said pointing again.

Finally I realized a splotchy piece of coral under the edge of the pool looked too smooth. I nodded, hoping that was it. It was. Ali made a hard, quick jab at the lump with his metal stick. It squirted black ink, and tentacles raced up Ali's arm. In a second he'd killed it.

He held it out to me, slimy and dripping ink, and said, "For you, it's very good to eat."

I must not have looked enthusiastic, because he said, "I will cook it for you tonight, and you will see."

"All right!" said David smiling. He and Alex had come over while Ali was killing it.

"What'd he say?" asked Alex.

"He said he'd cook us one," David answered. "They're really good, but kind of tough."

"Right, you love to eat octopuses, just like I'm not supposed to pick up stuff?" Alex sounded disgusted. "Well, you aren't fooling me, David Stewart. I'll pick up stuff if I want to and I bet you won't eat octopus, either."

He's going to get stung for sure, I thought. I figured it was time for us to go in. Besides Alex looked sunburnt and so did David, even though Mom had rubbed them both with sunscreen. I was probably getting burnt through my sunscreen, too.

"We'd better go in," I said to Ali.

"Wait a bit. I want to get a fish there first," and he pointed over a little way.

I'd been paying so much attention to watching Ali, I hadn't looked ahead. There was a split in the reef, and ocean water was pouring through like rapids in a river. Mida Creek! I hadn't realized we'd walked so far down the reef.

"Come," Ali said. "It will only take a little time."

He squatted down and started banging on the coral with his piece of metal. He knocked off a piece of coral and pulled out this gross ten-inch-long worm with legs down the side. He took out a piece of wood with fishing line wound around it and tied a hook on the line. Then he baited the hook with that ugly worm.

Ali didn't have a fishing pole or anything. He waded

into the edge of Mida Creek, whirled the hook around his head, and threw it out into the fast water.

"Don't you come here," he warned. "This is bad water."

He was right. Daddy warned us about it every time we came to the coast here. There was this long swampy inlet full of mangrove trees, and every high tide the ocean filled it with water. Every low tide, it emptied. So there was a lot of water moving there in a hurry. It poured in and out like a fast river and was only still for half an hour when the tide changed. It could sweep you away in a hurry. We were standing right next to where the water poured through the reef.

Ali looked as solid as a rock as he stood thigh-deep in the fast current and waited. He pulled the line in and threw it out again. This time he caught a shiny orange fish. He stuck it in his basket with the octopuses, and we headed back to the beach.

What happened when we got there made me forget all about asking Daddy to tell Alex not to pick stuff up.

As soon as we got to the beach, I stopped to pull my wet tennies off. My feet were shriveled up like raisins from being in the water so long. I'd just put one foot into the warm sand and was pulling off the other shoe when Sandy yelled at me. "Did you see Lisa Barnes?"

I looked up and yelled back, "No!" Hadn't they found Lisa yet?

Then Sandy yelled something else, but she was way up by the path and I couldn't hear her. So I started tugging at my shoe again.

A second later she and Traci were standing right in front of me, and they looked mad.

"Mom and Daddy made us look all over for Lisa Barnes," said Sandy. "It wrecked a whole morning! And you guys were out having fun."

"We had to walk all the way to that old Arab mosque ruin, down by where the mangroves start," said Traci.

"Did Daddy still rest?" I asked

"Yeah, but nobody else did," Traci said.

"That's OK then. Maybe the grown-ups found Lisa while you guys were looking," I said.

"Come on, Sandy. Let's go see if they did," said Traci, and they headed up the beach. Alex and David had come up behind me while Sandy and Traci were talking. As soon as Alex heard that Lisa was still gone, he took off for the house.

"We should tell Ali," David said and ran off to where Ali was cleaning the octopus down by the water.

I watched him go. Then all of a sudden, where our beach ends and the next one starts, someone walked out of the coral. It looked really funny until I remembered that there's a sort of cave where the sand runs underneath the black coral at the back of the beach. I squinted my eyes, but the person was gone. It was hard to see that far away, especially when the white sand makes you squint.

But I was almost sure it had been Lisa Barnes.

Chapter
Six

~~~~~~~~~~

Wow! Was she ever going to be in trouble. If the person I'd seen hide in the coral rock at the edge of our beach was Lisa, she had been hiding out right by the house all morning.

I looked up. Sandy and Traci had just reached the top of the beach. I took a big breath to yell at them, then stopped. Sandy and Traci would be really mad. If it was Lisa, she must have heard people calling her. She was going to be in enough trouble without me making it worse.

All of a sudden I had a plan. I'd go find Lisa and have her say she'd been lost somewhere else. That way she wouldn't get into so much trouble. Without stopping to think—or to ask God about it—I ran across the beach to the place I'd seen Lisa disappear. I didn't even pick up my shoes.

Higher on the beach, the dry sand pulled on my bare feet so it was hard to run. When I slowed down I could see the cave. A second later I was standing on the damp, packed sand of the entrance.

Clink, chink, clunk! The sound of the small rocks hitting the coral walls echoed loudly. I couldn't see anybody. The cave wasn't very high, but I still couldn't see to the back of it.

"Lisa! Lisa, are you in here?" I called.

One of the big flat rock crabs scuttled around a corner, making a scratchy rustling noise. I bent over and walked into the cave.

The sand felt cold and damp. My eyes were so used to the bright sun that I could hardly see. A drop of water fell off the ceiling onto my hot, bare back. More crabs scuttled into corners.

"Go away!"

The yell made me jump, but at least I knew now that Lisa *was* in this cave. That was definitely her voice.

"No, you come out," I answered. "We can say you went down the beach and got lost. Then everybody won't be so mad."

"Leave me alone. I don't need your dumb plans," Lisa yelled.

"Lisa, wise up," I said kind of irritated. "I just want to help you." I could see her now. A big blotch of sunlight came in from a tunnel up through the roof of the cave. Lisa was in the tunnel, halfway up. She was hanging onto her knee like it hurt.

"Go away!" she yelled. "Do I have to spell it? G-o a-wa-y. You made me cut myself trying to get away from you." She lifted her hand off her scraped knee to show me, then went on. "You tried to make me a slave driver, and now you want me to lie. I do not, n-o-t, *not,* need your help, Anika Scott."

A sound behind me made me jump. Someone else was coming into the cave.

"Anika?" that was David Stewart's voice. "Anika, how come you came running here? What happened?" A second later he'd crawled back to where I was, and he saw Lisa.

"How'd she get up there?" he asked me in a whisper.

I just shrugged, but Lisa yelled, "I'm not deaf. Don't talk about me! I got up here because you were chasing me. Go away!"

"We'll get your dad," I said and started backing out.

"No!" she said and started crying. It seemed like all she ever did was cry.

"OK, I'll help you get down then," I said.

"No! Just leave me alone!" she howled.

"Get Mrs. Barnes," I whispered to David, and he scooted out of the cave.

I sat down to wait. The wet sand felt cold on my legs. Lisa wouldn't look at me, but she didn't yell at me again, either. More drips fell from the ceiling and made patterns in the sand floor. I drew a circle in the sand around a drip mark and patted it away again. It seemed like it had been years since David left. Suddenly my stomach growled hungrily.

"Please, God . . . ," I whispered, then I didn't know what to say so I stopped. I felt bad about telling Lisa Barnes to lie.

I swallowed hard and said, "Lisa, I didn't really want to make you a liar. I just wanted to help. I want to be your friend."

She never even looked down, but I felt a little bit better anyway. I drew a butterfly around another drip. The wet sand stuck to my finger.

Clink, chink! Bits of rock rolled down out of the hole Lisa was in, and I looked up. She was climbing toward the hole in the cave roof.

"Hey, don't! Please wait, Lisa," I pleaded.

I could see a green tangle of vines and roots in the top of the hole. Already she could almost reach them.

I didn't want to lose her now, especially after I'd sent David for Mrs. Barnes. I braced my hands on both sides of the hole she'd gone up, then jerked back in pain. "Ouch!" That sharp coral had hurt.

Lisa heard me and looked down. She was halfway out already.

"Just go away!" she yelled and kicked a rock back at me. The rock bounced down past me, and Lisa's fancy

American running shoes disappeared up through the hole.

The coral bit into my bare feet, but I didn't stop climbing. By the time I got out the top, I couldn't see Lisa anywhere. But I could hear her in the thick tangled bush behind the coral.

"Lisa, wait!" I called, "It's full of snakes in the bush."

"Go away, liar! I hate you, and I hate your rotten country," she yelled. I could hear her keep on going straight in.

I wasn't lying. At the coast, the bush is *full* of poisonous snakes. Since I didn't have shoes on, I was a bit scared when I started picking my way off the sharp coral. Lisa had gone a lot faster with shoes on. Once I got into the bush there wasn't sharp coral underfoot, but the bush was thick and tangled and thorny. After a minute of pushing through the bush, I came to a path. I couldn't see Lisa, but her tracks showed on the sand. I ran after her, and in a couple of seconds I saw her ahead of me.

Just then a terrific pain shot up my leg. *Snake!* I thought and fell flat on my face. I was so scared when I fell that I couldn't even scream.

All I could think was that it only took five minutes to die if a mamba bit you. I waited for my vision to black out or for pain to fill up my whole body, but nothing happened except my foot kept on hurting.

Maybe I'm not dying after all, I thought. Finally I sat up and looked at my foot. There was a chunk of stick on it. I poked it. It was connected to my foot by this huge thorn in my heel. A wave of relief poured over me. Just a thorn. Who cared how big it was, it was just a thorn.

I reached down and took hold of the stick and tried to pull it off. Man, that *hurt!*

"Lisa!" I yelled, "Lisa Barnes, please come back!"

She didn't answer. A flash of fury at Lisa washed over me. *What an absolute, complete, and total despicable-horrible-gross jerk Lisa Barnes is!* I thought. *At least she could have stopped.*

After a second, I stood up and tried to walk down the path. I didn't want to sit there long enough to really meet a mamba. Not that they usually bother you, but thinking I'd been snakebit still had me scared. Unfortunately, every time I took a step the stick would get jerked and hurt like mad. I sat down and put my head in my hands.

It wasn't fair. I was trying to do what God wanted, and here I was with a huge thorn in my foot, all alone in bush full of snakes. Besides that, mosquitoes were whining around my ears and biting me, and my foot really hurt. Tears stung my eyes, and a second later I was really crying.

I rubbed my fists in my eyes and shook my head. No way was I going to be a crybaby. I tried to pull the stick off again. It hurt too much. I needed help.

"Mom!" I yelled. "Mommm!"

Nothing happened. I yelled again. Only silence and the whine of mosquitos answered me.

I'll probably die here before anybody finds me, I thought. That scared me even worse, and finally I thought of asking God for help. "Please, God, you've got to help me! Please!" I prayed.

I just had to get rid of that stick. This time I grabbed it with both my hands, shut my eyes tight, and yanked hard. It came halfway out, but it hurt so much it made my chest heave with sobs. I grabbed it again and jerked even harder. It came all the way out. I grabbed my foot and rocked back and forth, my teeth clenched. After a minute it stopped hurting so much.

"Thanks, God," I whispered. I stood up and picked up the stick. I wanted to show people how big the thorn was so they'd believe me. I started limping down the path, watching out for snakes.

A second later I heard people talking. I could tell what they were saying, but I couldn't see them because they weren't on the path. I don't know why, but instead of calling them I just stood still and listened.

"She was in there—she was!" It was David Stewart

talking. "Lisa Barnes was partway up that hole in the roof, and Anika was talking to her."

"Now don't worry your head, honey pie." Nobody could mistake that slow sugary voice for anybody but Mrs. Barnes. "We've just got to find where they have got to now. My, but there's a lot of mosquitoes in here. Ouch! These thorns are a nuisance. Why would Lisa ever come up here?"

"They have to be up here. There were no tracks coming out of the cave but David's," Mr. Barnes said in a sort of muted roar. "Hush and keep your eyes open. If Lisa doesn't hear us she won't have a chance to run off again."

Right. You could have heard him a mile away. In fact, it sounded like more than three people by all the noise they made, and it seemed like they were going to go right past me.

"Hey! I'm here!" I yelled.

"Lisa?" bellowed Mr. Barnes.

"No, it's me, Anika. I'm here on a path."

David and Alex got to me first, then Traci and Sandy. Mom and the Barneses took longer to get through the bush. Everybody but Daddy was there.

"Is Lisa here, too, Anika?" Mom asked, still pushing her way through. Nobody had even noticed I was hurt.

"No, but look." I showed her the bottom of my foot.

95

Mom rushed over and held my foot to look at it. It was all bloody and dirty and everybody stared, which made me feel better.

"I don't know where Lisa is," I said kind of hopping on one foot to keep my balance. "She was ahead of me on the path, but she got away when I stepped on this." I waved the stick. "She never even stopped."

Mom wasn't impressed. "Maybe she didn't know you hurt yourself, Anika. Besides, you should know better than to go into coral or into the bush with bare feet. I don't know what we're going to do with you."

"But Mom, I wanted to help Lisa."

Everybody was still asking questions, most of which I didn't know the answers to, when we started down the path. I walked on the toes of my hurt foot, slowly. *Maybe Lisa really didn't know I was hurt,* I thought. Then I remembered I'd only yelled at her to stop. I hadn't said why. Maybe she was too far away to hear by the time I'd yelled for Mom. Gradually my anger at Lisa started to go away again. Besides, she was going to be in enough trouble for hiding all morning.

A few minutes later the path led us into the clearing around the house.

Daddy was still sitting in a lawn chair out front. "Joey," he called, "your daughter came back a few minutes ago and went into the house."

Mom had to fix my foot up, but I could hear Mr. Barnes yelling at Lisa in the front room.

When I finally limped out with a bandage on my heel, Sandy and Traci were looking righteous because they were making lunch. They didn't have to look so holy, because it turned out Daddy had told them to do it. It was just hot dogs anyway, and anybody can boil a hot dog.

When Lisa was marched out to lunch between her parents, she looked like a prisoner of war being taken to be executed. Her face was red and puffy from crying. She wouldn't look at anybody.

"Lisa would like to apologize to all of you," Mr. Barnes said.

Lisa muttered something that sounded sort of like "Sorry."

"Lisa! You apologize properly. You've caused every one of us a lot of trouble today." Mr. Barnes's voice seemed to fill up the room and push at your face.

"Joey, let her be. Can't you see that she's about worn to a frazzle?" pleaded Mrs. Barnes.

"No, she will apologize!"

But Lisa twisted out of his grip and ran to our room. We could hear her crying.

"She can apologize later," said Daddy. "Come and sit down, Joey." Daddy didn't say it loud, but you could tell from his voice that he didn't want Mr. Barnes to go after Lisa. I was sure glad he was my dad and not Mr. Barnes. I looked at him sitting there and loved him so much it almost hurt. If only he'd hurry up and get better.

Daddy asked the blessing for the meal, and he prayed for Lisa, but he never asked God about making him well at all. Nobody said much. I noticed that Daddy only ate one bite of his hot dog. About halfway through, Mrs. Barnes went and got Lisa. She came out and sat there, looking down and picking at her hot dog.

"Well, I know what I'm going to do this afternoon," Mom said. "I'm going to take a nap. In fact, I think most of us could use one." She smiled at Lisa and said, "This has been a bard horning for everyone."

Sometimes I think she does it on purpose.

Anyway, everybody laughed and that made me feel better.

I finished reading my book, *The Voyage of the Dawn Treader,* that afternoon. Then I actually went to sleep, which I don't usually do.

"Come on, Anika, wake up," Sandy was saying.

I sat up feeling as limp as melted cheese and rubbed my eyes.

"Come on. It's high tide. We're going swimming. Get your stuff." Sandy just had her head stuck in the door.

As soon as she saw I'd heard, she left. She was already in her swimsuit.

No way did I want to miss the first high tide swim. I got out of bed in a hurry. *Ow!* My foot *hurt* when it touched the floor. It felt better by the time I had my suit on, and I made sure I wasn't limping when I walked out the door. Even so, I had to beg and beg to get Mom to let me go swimming.

"OK, Anika, if you insist," she said. "On one condition. You know that ocean water can cause infections. You can swim if you promise you'll soak your foot in hot water and Epsom salts afterward. It's your foot, and infected puncture wounds are no joke."

"OK, OK, I promise!" I said and headed out the door. Because of the fuss with my foot, everyone but Mom was at the beach ahead of me. The beach at Bilge Water isn't the best beach around. It's too steep for the waves to be really good, and there are round, light red chunks of coral in the sand, about as big as your hand. These wash back and forth in the waves and bash you on the shins.

I didn't care. It was great to be in the ocean at high tide. I swam out past the breakers and floated on my back. The waves pushed up under me, then dropped me down their backs with a rocking swoop. Every now and then, one would swat me in the face with a small splash just for the fun on it. I was lying there with my eyes half-shut, enjoying the ride, when, *wham!* a huge hand landed on my face and shoved me under.

"Ha, ha, ha! I got you good, Anika," boomed Mr. Barnes as I came up, spluttering. I gave him a sick grin, did a surface dive, and swam underwater away from him. He didn't catch me again, but he was dunking everyone. He even dunked Mom, and she hates that. I mean she can swim, sort of, but she hates getting her face wet and she's always a little bit scared.

What with playing in the waves and watching out for Mr. Barnes, I hardly noticed Lisa. I guess she stayed on the beach most of the time. I really felt sorry for her with a dad like Mr. Barnes. Daddy had stayed back at the house resting, and I missed him. He usually played in the water with us.

On the way back up to the house, Sandy and Traci caught up to me. "Wait till you see what we did to Lisa's bed," said Traci.

Sandy nodded. "She'll be sorry for making us walk all the way down to the mangrove trees, when she was right by the house the whole time."

"What did you do?" I asked, feeling all weird inside.

"You know those really sharp three-cornered burrs? Well, we picked about a hundred and stuck them in her sleeping bag. See?" said Traci, showing me her pricked fingers.

"But what if you make the Barneses go back to the States like Mom said, because of Lisa?"

"I don't care!" said Traci. "Mr. Barnes dunked me three times."

Sandy wouldn't look at me. I could tell the whole thing was mostly Traci's idea.

By the time I'd gotten showered and soaked my foot, it was supper time. Mom had bought the fish from the fisherman who came by this morning, and, boy, was it good. Ali kept his word and brought out a little dish of deep-fried octopus.

Mr. Barnes took some and Alex said, "Gross, you're gonna eat that!?"

He grinned and took a bite and made a big deal of chewing it, saying, "Mmmmmmmmm," really loud.

Alex stared at him with his eyes all screwed up. Then, believe it or not, Lisa actually said something. "Don't be a geek, Alex. I've had octopus at home at Nykono's."

Lisa sure thinks she's hot stuff and knows every-thing, I thought. I took some octopus, too, though. It tasted good, but it was chewy.

After supper we played Monopoly, but I kept thinking about Lisa. I ended up landing on Park Place and was out of the game about halfway through. I went back to our room and tried to start reading a book called *The Silver Chair.* It's part of a series of books by a writer named C.S. Lewis, all about some kids and another world they find, and a huge, majestic lion named Aslan. I loved the books! I'd just finished *The Voyage of the Dawn Treader,* which was the book that came just before the one I was starting to read. But I couldn't pay attention to my book, either. A Bible verse kept bugging me. You know, the one about loving your enemies and being kind to those who are mean to you?

I looked out into the other room. Sandy and Traci were still playing Monopoly. Lisa must have been in her mom's room or somewhere. I opened up her sleeping bag and started picking out the burrs. Some of them were really stuck in the cloth. Pretty soon there was a little heap of them on top of Lisa's suitcase.

I'd finished one spot and was just starting on another one when somebody yelled, "Hey!" right behind me.

I dropped a burr and swung around. Lisa was there staring at me.

"Some friend you are," she said and then yelled, "Mom, come here and see what this geek is doing to my bed."

Mrs. Barnes and everybody else crowded into the room and stared at me.

"But, but, I didn't . . . ," I said and stopped. I wasn't a tattletale.

"Anika, you go to our room," a stern voice said. It

was Daddy. "Sandy and Traci, clean out that sleeping bag. If there's even one burr left in there, you'll have cause to be sorry."

In Mom and Dad's room, I just sat there and let them lecture me. There was no use saying anything. I just picked at some dirt under my thumbnail. Every time I tried to do something right, things just got worse. Daddy started accusing me of being rebellious because I wouldn't explain to him why I'd done it. I felt even worse, because halfway through he sort of stopped and sat down. I could tell he was feeling sicker.

"Now you apologize to Lisa and her parents," Mom said, after an anxious glance at Daddy. "Tomorrow is Sunday, and we all need to be ready to worship God together. This kind of tension is not helpful." She sounded sad and disappointed. I could hardly stand it.

By the time I finally got out of there, the other kids were in bed. I said I was sorry to the Barneses and went to bed, too. Nobody said a word to me when I came into the room, even though I could tell they were all awake.

I was almost asleep when I heard Sandy get out of bed and sneak out of the room, but I was too sleepy to pay much attention.

The next morning, I went down to the beach again just before dawn. The wide, quiet ocean made me feel better right away. Even if it seemed like everything went wrong, I could tell God still loved me.

I started running along in the edge of the water, where it touches the beach. Glittering sprays of sea water went up from my feet. The cool splashes hit my face and felt good. They tasted salty. These little black-and-white birds were wading in the edge of the water. They'd fly up and go a little way and land. Then when I got close again they'd do it all over. They came with me a long way down the beach.

It took me a lot longer to get back because I poked along looking in the sticks and seaweed and stuff that was along the top of the beach. I found a perfect reefing stick, round and hard and light white wood—just the way I like them. There were bunches of frayed-looking coconuts, little parts of thongs, cuttlefish bones, mangrove seeds, and other interesting stuff. I'd always wanted to find one of those big green glass balls they say float all the way from Japan, but I didn't that day.

By the time I got back, everybody was already at the breakfast table. I went in the house with a sigh. I sure hoped today would be better than yesterday.

Chapter
Seven

~~~~~~~~~~~~~~~~~~~~~~~~~~~~~~~~~

"Aunt Hazel, Anika's here," Traci yelled as soon as I walked through the door.

"Tell her to hurry up and eat and get ready. She's late," Mom answered.

"Hurry-up-and-eat-and-get-ready-you're-late!" Traci yelled in my face, grinning like a hyena.

I made a face at her and went and grabbed a banana. Its thin skin felt cool on my hand. I'd forgotten it was Sunday.

"Anika, as soon as you've eaten that, go and put a dress on," Mom said as she walked back in from the kitchen.

"Why do I have to put a dress on? We're having church here just with us, aren't we?" I absolutely hate wearing dresses. I don't think I've ever liked a single dress I've owned.

"No," Mom said. "Do you remember Hasan from the Bible school? He's started a little church not far from here. We'll be going there."

"Do we have to?" I moaned. That meant hours of listening to boring Swahili, sitting in hard wooden seats, and sweating. "Can't we kids stay home?"

"No, you can't," Mom snapped. It seemed like she was upset about something other than me because she walked off without even giving me a lecture.

When I went into the bedroom to get dressed, Sandy was the only one there. She was already dressed.

"Anika, I've got to talk to you." It seemed like everybody had to talk to me.

"What?" I snapped. After all, she had let me get all the blame for the burrs in Lisa's bed.

"You know I got up in the middle of the night?" she asked.

I just nodded.

"Well, I was going to tell Mom and Dad that Traci and I had put those burrs in Lisa's bed. But I never told them. I mean, like, I went to their door and all, but I never went in. Anika, Daddy was sick again last night. He was throwing up and everything."

I forgot all about getting dressed and sat down with a plop on my bed.

"Sandy, Anika, hurry up!" It was Mom calling. How could she just keep going like nothing was wrong? She sounded like she meant it about hurrying, though. Sandy went out right away, and I pulled my dress over my head. At least we didn't have to wear shoes and socks. I stuffed my feet into my thongs, grabbed my Bible, and went out.

Daddy was all ready to go, too, and he didn't look any sicker than yesterday. I wondered if Sandy had imagined him being sick.

I guess Mr. Barnes thought Daddy looked sicker, though. He boomed, "Kevin, you look a bit peaked this morning."

How can he make everything he says sound like an announcement? I wondered.

Mr. Barnes was still talking, "I noticed you didn't eat breakfast this morning, either. Why don't you stay home and rest today?"

Sandy and I looked at each other.

"No, Joey," Daddy answered. I let my breath out in kind of a sigh. "Hazel and I have already hashed this through. I gave my word that I'd be there to preach today, and I won't go back on that. I have promised Hazel I won't make any more commitments like this one until I'm completely well, but I do feel I've got to go this time. I've already committed myself. I would appreciate your prayers that what I say is effective."

"Well, if that's how you feel about it, let's pray right now," Mr. Barnes said. He prayed about Daddy saying the right things. Then he prayed about Daddy getting better.

Maybe Mr. Barnes does have a few good points, I thought.

It turned out that the "church" didn't have a church building yet. It was only about fifteen adults and a bunch of little kids.

Alex Barnes stared for a second, with his eyebrows kind of frowning, and then asked really loud, "Is this it? Where's the church?"

He looked so stunned, I couldn't help laughing. Lisa gave me a really dirty look.

Hasan came over right then, and Mom started introducing him to the Barneses. Hasan must have heard Alex's comment, because when he shook Alex's hand he said, "The church is not buildings, it is the people of God coming to worship God. Is that not so, Mrs. Scott?"

We all sat in a hot, sandy, open space, and I thought about what Hasan had said. All the adults had agreed, so it must be right. "The people of God coming to worship God." That sounded neat. All of a sudden I had a picture in my head of God's people, all over the whole world, who were worshipping that Sunday. Different languages, different places . . . but, if Hasan was right, all one church.

I looked around and wasn't mad about having to come to Hasan's church anymore. It was neat to be in such an interesting part of God's church.

I glanced around and noticed that we were near some African houses. They were made out of chunks of coral and had tin roofs. There were coconut palms behind the houses and a bunch of brightly colored chickens pecking around. People were still coming toward the church. Some looked as though they'd walked a long way.

All the kids sat on the ground, except for us. That made me feel kind of funny. I mean, I knew the church people were having all of their guests sit on chairs to be polite, but that meant that some of the women were sitting on the ground.

First Hasan stood up. I couldn't understand everything he said. I know Swahili, but sermon Swahili is hard. They use big words and fancy grammar. I could tell he was talking about us being honored guests, and then he said something about the Barnes family giving him much joy because they were new workers with him for the Lord. He kept talking for ages.

I wasn't really paying attention. There was this ant lion hole in the sand right by my chair leg—I kept watching it and hoping for an ant to fall in.

Suddenly Mom and Sandy stood up, and I realized we were supposed to be standing to sing a hymn.

"Anika, pay attention," Mom whispered.

Hasan hummed a note, and we all started in singing

"God Is So Good" in Swahili. Everybody except Mr. Barnes, that is. He bellowed it out in English at the top of his lungs.

After about four more hymns, Daddy got up to preach. He talked about serving God even when it will cost you a lot. I wondered if he meant preaching today. I looked around; most of the people were listening closely. Maybe it *was* worth it for Daddy to come preach.

When Daddy was done, Hasan got up and started talking again. Like before, I didn't really listen. A fly landed on my cheek, and I brushed it off, but it just kept hopping over my hand and landing again. A sweat trickle ran down my back.

I noticed Lisa kind of hitch herself over in a funny way, so I watched her for a minute. Four times she tried to skootch her chair away from the African man on the other side of her. She couldn't get far, because her chair was already right against her dad's chair. Mr. Barnes finally glared at her, and she held still.

"Khaaah, Khaaa!" I suddenly noticed a horrible gurgling cough noise. Actually, I'd been hearing it all morning, but not really paying attention to it. I looked around and saw a girl not much older than me who was holding a baby. That awful cough was coming from the baby. The girl thumped her baby on the back, and it spit up some stuff. My stomach lurched. Then the baby coughed that horrible cough again. I frowned, wondering if the baby was going to die. The girl's face looked worried, but she was still listening to Hasan. I tried to listen, too, and decided he was preaching Daddy's sermon all over again.

I twisted in my chair to see the sick baby better and crossed my legs. That meant that my right leg stuck to my left leg instead of the chair. Sweat trickled down the back of my knee, making it itch like crazy. The thought of diving into a cool ocean wave was almost too much to bear.

Finally Hasan finished the closing prayer. Everybody said, "Aaaaaammmm," and stood up.

As soon as everybody stood up, I headed for Mom, but one of the ladies grabbed my hand to greet me. Her hand felt strong and calloused, and she held on tight and quizzed me about how I was and how Mom was. That's the polite thing to do. When she asked about my father, I didn't know what to say. Finally I just said, "He's well." I didn't want to explain everything. Besides, how do you say "hepatitis" in Swahili?

By this time, Mom was getting further away. I pushed my way toward her, then I had to wait for ages while people greeted her.

"Mom," I hissed, pulling at the hand that wasn't

being shaken. I just had to ask her if we could help that sick baby.

"Anika, don't interrupt," was all I got for my efforts. By the time she quit talking and turned to me, the baby was nowhere in sight.

"We can't fix everything," she said when I explained. "You're right, though, the baby does seem sick. I'll ask Hasan what the situation is. Maybe we can help."

Daddy came over right then to say that Hasan had invited us for dinner. I almost died. We'd end up sitting for hours while somebody killed a chicken and made a whole meal, and we'd have to be polite in Swahili the whole time.

I gave Mom this really pleading look, but she never even saw me. It didn't matter, though.

"No," she was saying, "thank you very much, but Mr. Scott has been ill and needs to rest."

I think that's the only time I was almost glad Daddy was sick.

The cars were almost too hot to touch. Alex and David piled into our car with Traci and Sandy, so I ended up riding back in the Barneses' car with Lisa.

"Mom, those people stink!" Lisa said as soon as we started. "I thought I was going to pass out from the smell of that man next to me."

"Lisa! That's enough," Mr. Barnes bellowed. "We

come all the way to Africa to teach people about God's love, and all you can say is that they stink?"

"Well, they do," said Lisa, and she shut up.

She was right, but I'd never thought much about it. I did on the way home, though, because no one said anything at all after Lisa shut up. I decided maybe the people smelled because they don't have running water, so getting clean is a lot harder. Then I remembered hearing that the workers on one mission station used to wash clothes together and then sort them out by smell.

Maybe they think we stink, too, I thought and shook my head. It's hard to try to look at the world from inside someone else's head.

As soon as we got home, Lisa went into the shower room and took the longest shower ever. It was like she was trying to wash off the smell of the African church.

At lunch Sandy said, "Mom, can we go swimming?"

"It's low tide, remember?" Daddy answered for her.

"Can you take us over to the big beach this afternoon then?" Traci said. The big beach has a longer stretch of sand, so you can swim even when it's half tide. It's about a mile away from Bilge Water.

Mom looked at Daddy. He looked pale and tired, but he said, "We don't want to spoil this trip for the kids, Hazel."

Mom said she'd take us if the Barneses wouldn't, but that it would have to be a bit later on after lunch. Sandy and Traci cheered, but I just looked at Daddy. He didn't eat much lunch at all and left the table early to go lie down on a lawn chair out front in the shade.

Somehow I didn't feel like going down to the beach to poke around the tide pools. I sat out front with Daddy and read. He slept most of the time.

"Last one in the car is a rotten egg," Mr. Barnes yelled out the door, later that afternoon. "Tide's in, let's get a wiggle on." Daddy woke up with a jerk, then sighed and shut his eyes again. I felt like kicking Mr. Barnes.

I went in the room to put my swimsuit on and passed Traci and Sandy coming out. They were giggling together about something. Alex and David were grabbing their towels off the clothesline when I went out to the car.

Everybody except Daddy packed into the Barneses' car. I ended up wedged right by Lisa. She stared out the window and wouldn't even look at me. It made my stomach hurt. *Why can't this be peaceful and fun like other trips to the coast?* I wondered.

The Indian Ocean made up for the uncomfortable ride. It's impossible to be sad or worried when you're playing in big breakers. They don't give you time. Before we went into the water, Mom asked everybody to come over so she could talk to us. Lisa ignored her and kept walking toward the water, but she was behind Mom so Mom didn't notice.

"This beach is close to Mida Creek inlet," Mom said. "Make sure you don't swim out too far, because when the tide turns that current is only two hundred yards off the beach. It could sweep you right out into the open ocean."

Mida Creek is the same current where Ali had caught those fish, and it is dangerous. I already knew that. This was the same old lecture we got every time we came to the big beach. As Mom talked, I watched the waves—they were super! I could hardly wait for Mom to get done so we could run for the water.

Close to the water, the sand was smooth and hard; I loved the way it felt under my feet. When the tail end of a wave hit me on the shins, I took some high gallops and dove straight through the front of an incoming wave. The cool, rough water cleaned all the dirt, sweat, and worry off of me. A few seconds later I was chest-deep, watching for the next wave.

I jumped it backwards, and it threw me up high and swatted me over the head and shoulders. I caught the next wave, swimming like mad just in front of the crest. It broke and buried my body in boiling foam and rushed me up onto the beach.

That afternoon was really fun.

That night, on the other hand, was one of the worst nights of my whole life.

"We must get Kevin to the hospital," Mr. Barnes's voice brought me fully awake. When we'd come back from the beach, I'd been more than ready for bed and had fallen asleep quickly. Now I sat up, startled by Mr. Barnes's voice, and blinked my eyes. I could see Lisa and Traci standing in the doorway of our room. Sandy wasn't in the room.

"What's going on?" I asked.

"Your dad is really sick," said Traci, sounding half worried and half excited.

I rushed to the door in time to hear Mom say, "Joey, those hospitals are dangerous. AIDS is widespread here, and there's a real risk of exposure." She paused, then went on, her voice strained and full of concern, "Maybe I could get through to Dr. Bishop. They were supposed to be at Diani Beach."

"We don't even have a telephone," Mrs. Barnes wailed.

"Maybe there's one at that duka where we got lost. If not, I'll go all the way to Diani Beach to get Bishop— except I don't know the way. You can't leave Kevin, can you?" Mr. Barnes asked Mom.

Sandy had been standing by Mom. Suddenly she spoke up, "I know the way. I do, Mom. I really do. Please let me show him."

Mom looked doubtful and finally said, "Well, I can't go, and you have been good at remembering directions all your life, Sandy. Are you absolutely sure you know the way?"

"I do! Really, I do!" Sandy insisted.

Mr. Barnes said he'd trust her, so finally Mom said she didn't see that she had much choice. I wanted to go, too, but Mom knew I'm no good at directions. So, even though I'm oldest, she made me stay home. We all prayed together, then Mr. Barnes and Sandy left.

Mom wouldn't even let me come in with her to help take care of Daddy, so I ended up curled up in a knot in my bed. Traci came and sat by me and, after a while, so did Lisa. I just stayed curled up in a knot.

Just let Daddy be OK, I prayed over and over in my head. *I'll go to the States or anything! Just let Daddy be OK.*

Mrs. Barnes came in and put her hand on me, "Honey, your daddy is God's man, and I'm sure God'll be looking after him. Now I want y'all to get some sleep."

She made Traci and Lisa go back to bed and turned

off the light. Just thinking about Daddy and how selfish I'd been about not going back to the States made me start crying. I stuffed my head under my pillow, because it's so embarrassing when people know you're crying. All I could think about was what Daddy had said at church about giving up things to serve God.

"Please, God, don't make him give up his life. I need him," I prayed.

That made me start crying again. I'd been too selfish even to give up living in Kenya. Well, I wasn't too selfish anymore. Right then I decided I'd be willing to live in the States forever, if that's what God wanted. If Daddy was willing to serve God even if he died, I wanted to serve God that way, too.

I thought about never seeing Kilimanjaro again, or dawn over the Indian Ocean. I thought about never seeing giraffes walking in graceful swaying groups across the golden grass. No acacia trees, or dukas with samosas . . . I started crying just thinking about it. But thinking about Daddy dying was even worse. Finally I'd cried so much I didn't have any tears left. So I went to sleep.

I woke up the next morning with a splitting headache. My eyes were all stuck shut. It took me a second to remember what was wrong, and I sat up with a jerk.

Sandy was back in her bed sleeping, but Lisa and Traci were both gone.

I jumped out of bed and ran into the main room. Mrs. Barnes was sitting there reading her Bible.

"Where's Mom?" I practically yelled at her. "Is Daddy all right? Did they find Dr. Bishop?"

"Well, hi, honey," she drawled, "I'm glad to see you've had a good long sleep."

Her slow talking had never frustrated me so much. Why couldn't she get to the point? "How about Daddy?" I asked again.

"Now just you take it easy. Your Uncle Joey brought Dr. Bishop back here last night, and your father is doing much better," she said. "In fact, he's asleep right now and so is your poor tired mother. You can go and see your daddy when he wakes up, if it's OK with Dr. Bishop."

"Where's Dr. Bishop?"

She pointed toward the front of the house, and I ran off before she had time to drawl another slow sentence at me.

Dr. Bishop was sitting in one of the deck chairs there. I hadn't seen him for ages, but I'd always liked him. He's a little man with gray hair and the friendliest brown eyes.

"Oh, hello, Anika," he said as soon as he saw me.

"Your dad is OK for now, but I wanted to talk to you about something."

That sounded serious. I just nodded and waited.

"Don't look at me with your big brown eyes like that," he said, a smile curving at his lips. "I'm not going to eat you. I just wanted to ask for your help to give your dad a better chance to recover."

"I'll do anything," I blurted.

He looked at me thoughtfully for a minute. "Well, I really am glad to hear that, Anika, because I know that your mother and dad have been reluctant to go back to North America. A big part of their reluctance has been you and your love for Africa. But things have changed with your dad now, and I think he and your mom need to know they can make the best decision for all of you."

I swallowed hard, and my head started hurting again. So did my heart. We were going back to the States—I was almost sure of it now. We were leaving my home, and we might never come back . . . and I had to act as though that was OK.

"I—I already decided last night that it would be OK to move to the States, if that was what Daddy needed," I said, my voice coming out kind of choked.

"Good girl," Dr. Bishop answered. He has the warmest voice. . . . It almost made me feel better. "Will you

tell your mom and dad what you've decided?" I just nodded and he said, "Off you go, then, and enjoy your last
day at the coast. Nobody's leaving here until tomorrow.
Your dad should be feeling a bit better by then, and I'll
be driving your car."

"What about your vacation?" I asked.

"Sometimes we have to give up things in the Lord's
service, but I'm not worried. God takes care of us. Whatever we give up to him in obedience, he gives back
eventually in blessing. Now off with you."

Even Dr. Bishop is talking about giving up things, I
thought as I walked toward the beach. It was almost
noon, but somehow I didn't feel like eating—or seeing
Mrs. Barnes again.

I stood on the top of the hill above the beach looking
at all the colors in the ocean at low tide. *I might never
ever see this again,* I thought, and tears stung the back
of my eyes.

"OK," I prayed right out loud, "I'll go. Just please let
Daddy get better." Then I gulped and changed that, too.
"I mean please let Daddy get better if that's what you
want. I know I'm supposed to pray that, but I still want
Daddy better."

All of a sudden I felt really peaceful inside, almost
happy. A verse came into my head, and this time it
wasn't nagging. In fact, it made me feel good: "Let God

have all your worries and cares. He is always thinking about you and watching everything that concerns you." I could feel God's love all around me.

I turned around and walked back up to the house to see if Mom and Dad were awake yet. I was ready to talk to them now.

Chapter Eight

When I got back to the house, Dr. Bishop wasn't out front anymore. Inside I could hear adults' voices. I went in and found Mom and Mrs. Barnes sitting at the table, talking. I could hear Dr. Bishop and Daddy talking in the other room.

I went over and hugged Mom, and she hugged me back hard.

"Dr. Bishop said that Daddy is OK?" I said it like it was a question.

Mom nodded. "God is so good to have put Dr. Bishop at the coast right when we needed him," she said. Then she looked at Mrs. Barnes and added, "I can't tell you how much that man has meant to us and to many others. He is literally a godsend."

I thought about what Dr. Bishop had said about getting things back when you give something up and wondered if he knew what people thought of him. It would be good to have people think of me that way sometime, no matter what it cost. *I think I'd like to be a doctor someday,* I thought. Then I remembered what I had to say to Mom and Dad.

"Mom, I need to talk to you and Daddy together as soon as I can, OK?" I asked.

She nodded and smiled at me, then said, "Go and sis if soar yeeter is awake."

I laughed right out loud, "Seems like you haven't done that for ages, Mom. Sure, I'll go see if my yeeter is awake. Do you want me to wake her up if she isn't? Where are Traci and Lisa? I haven't seen them any-where?"

"Mr. Barnes took them and David and Alex on a long walk down the beach this morning so we could sleep," she looked back at Mrs. Barnes. "Both you and Joey have been very good to us. I appreciate it so much."

Mrs. Barnes smiled and started to answer, but I didn't hear much of it because I was halfway into the bedroom before she got started.

Sandy was sitting up, looking really sleepy.

"Hi!" I said, "Dr. Bishop says that Daddy's OK for now."

"Good. I don't even remember getting back. I must have gone to sleep in the car or something, and Uncle Joey carried me in."

"Uncle Joey?!" I asked. "Since when is Mr. Barnes Uncle Joey?"

"He's nice to me, and I like him," Sandy said, sounding a little defensive. "Besides, he practically saved Daddy's life last night by getting Dr. Bishop."

"I suppose . . . ," I said real slow. "Anyway, Dr. Bishop said something to me I wanted to tell you before we see Mom and Daddy. He said that Daddy needs to go to the States, and he doesn't want us worrying them by fussing about it anymore."

"Oh," Sandy answered and was quiet for a minute thinking about it. "That was mostly you anyway."

At first I wanted to get mad at her, but she was right. It *was* mostly me.

"Well anyway," I said, "Daddy's awake now, too. I could hear him talking to Dr. Bishop when I came in. I've got to tell him and Mom that I'm not going to try to make us stay in Kenya anymore."

"Do you know if we're going home today?" Sandy asked when I was halfway out the door.

"No, tomorrow—if we do what Dr. Bishop wants, anyway." I answered.

"Hey, wait," she called, but I wanted to talk to Mom and Daddy and get it over with. Especially because I was still so sad whenever I thought about leaving Kenya. I didn't want to change my mind. Nobody was out in the big room, so I went and knocked on Mom and Daddy's door.

When Mom called, "Come in," I stopped for a second and thought frantically, *Maybe I can ask them if I can stay in Kenya with Stewarts. Maybe they'd let me.* Then I remembered what Dr. Bishop had said about not making things hard for Daddy. I sighed and went in.

Daddy did look sick. I mean, hepatitis makes you look yellowish, but now he was pale under his tan, so it looked even worse. I ran and hugged him, and right that minute what I had to say didn't seem so hard anymore.

I let go and sat up on the bed and looked at them both.

"Mom, Daddy, I'm sorry for making things so hard for you about going back to the States. I'm ready to go now. I guess I thought I could tell God what was best for me instead of listening to what he wanted."

I looked down.

Daddy reached out and took my hand, "Anika, I'm proud of you. This isn't easy for you, but God's will is always best even if we don't understand it."

"We know that all that happens to us is working for our good if we love God and are fitting into his plans," Mom quoted. I knew that verse; it was Romans 8:28. Mom smiled and went on, "That verse has really meant a lot to me since your father got sick. It's so hard for me to see the good in this."

Daddy reached for Mom with his other hand and

said, "You know what verse has meant a lot to me? Psalm 27:13 where it says, 'I am expecting the Lord to rescue me again, so that once again I will see his goodness to me here in the land of the living.' See, already something good has come from it."

He smiled at me, and I felt warm—I knew he meant me and what I'd learned.

"Mom, Daddy, can I come in?" It was Sandy. Mom told her yes, and she came to sit on Daddy's bed.

"Now that we're all here, let's just put our future in God's hands," Daddy said. So we did. We held hands around the bed and took turns praying.

I felt so happy and clean inside. I didn't feel like anything in the whole world could wreck that peace. I was sure that if I felt that good with God, nothing could really go wrong. I felt happy—and suddenly I was hungry, too. None of us had eaten anything yet that day.

"Can I make lunch?" I asked. "Is anybody else hungry?"

"I'm starved," Sandy said. "Come on, I'll help you."

It turned out we didn't have to make anything, though. Mrs. Barnes had done it already.

"I don't know exactly whether I should call this here meal lunch or supper," she said. "It's so late that maybe it's lupper. Whatever, I want y'all to eat up. It'll make y'all feel better if your innards aren't so bare."

The idea of bare innards made me want to giggle—

especially the way she said it, "bayer innurds"—but the soup and grilled cheese sandwiches looked great.

"I've made up a special bowl of clear soup here for Kevin," she said. "Dr. Bishop said that's the right thing for him, so if one of y'all could take it in to him I'd be much obliged."

Just then Mr. Barnes came back with all the other kids and said, "Hey, isn't it a bit early for supper? Ha, ha, ha. It's only three-thirty."

Sandy ignored how loud and stupid he sounded and ran up to him. "Uncle Joey, Uncle Joey, Daddy's OK . . . but we're going back to the States."

"Is Kevin really going to be fine?" he asked, looking at Dr. Bishop, who had also come in.

"It seems so, but I would feel much more comfortable if he had further tests done in North America. He's had amebiasis as well, and I'm afraid the liver involvement may not be simple infectious hepatitis."

"Amebi-what's-it, eh? Well, whatever that means, I'm sure you know what you're talking about, ha, ha," Mr. Barnes boomed. "I tell you, man, was I ever glad to find you last—"

Suddenly Lisa interrupted. What she'd heard had finally sunk in. "You mean these people get to go back to America while we're stuck here? Anika Scott gets to go back, and I can't?!"

Her voice was really high and angry.

"Lisa, settle down," Mr. Barnes said. "You know Anika doesn't want to go."

"It's just not fair!" she yelled.

"Hush, child!" It was her mother. "Are you trying to teach God his business?"

For a second I thought Lisa was going to run away and cry again, but Mr. Barnes was glaring at her, so she sat down instead.

"Well, well, well," said Dr. Bishop, looking hard at Lisa, then at her parents. "I think I'll prescribe an afternoon swim. It'll be high tide before long, and there's still three hours till dark. I think everyone could use the relaxation."

Alex and David both yelled and jumped around, and Traci was smiling.

"Oh, Traci and David, I've got good news for you," said Dr. Bishop. "I'd forgotten in all the confusion, but I'd intended to drive up here later in the week. We had a phone call from your folks, and your grandmother is unexpectedly recovering. Your folks will be back by the end of the week."

Now Traci really did smile, and David kept asking Dr. Bishop questions he couldn't answer about Aunt Bea and Uncle Paul. I guess he'd missed them more than I thought.

Anyway, everybody started getting ready for swimming, and I felt happier than I had for ages. It was great not to be fighting inside myself about going to the States anymore. Lisa didn't bother me anymore, either. If God could help me feel OK about going to the States, he could sure help me be nice to her.

I guess I still bothered her though, because when I asked if she wanted to use my tube in the waves, she wouldn't even look at me.

We were going to the big beach again, so we tied the inner tubes on top of the Barneses' car, and we all crammed in. Mom and Dr. Bishop had decided to stay with Daddy, so we all fit—sort of. Sandy's elbow was right in my ribs, and I ended up with David's bony little behind perched on my knees. It hurt when he kept hopping up and down to talk across Sandy to Alex.

I was really glad to get out of that car. All of us made a wild run for the water. Everybody except Lisa and Mr. and Mrs. Barnes, anyway. I left my tube for Lisa, in case she wanted it. The Barneses must have wanted to let Mom and Dad rest, because we stayed for ages. I rode waves till they started getting smaller. The sun was low, too. *Must be almost time to go home,* I thought.

I stood up all dizzy and sandy from riding a wave in, when Alex and David came swooshing in on another wave and hit me in the shins. They were both in tubes, trying to keep locked together and giggling like mad.

I grabbed one tube and said, "Hold on," and tried to pull them out through the waves. We kept getting knocked over. It was great. The tube felt sticky and sandy under my arm. My mouth was full of the ocean's salty taste. My ears were full of the waves' crash and hiss and little boys' giggles. David had this really silly high giggle that made me laugh, too.

I didn't pull them very far out, because Mida Creek is right there. I just pulled them to where the last big waves were breaking. Even so, we could feel the pull of Mida Creek. It was easy to end up farther down the beach than where you started if you didn't watch it.

A wave almost dumped us. I saw Sandy and Traci dive under it and wait for the next one, which they caught. That one grabbed the inner tubes and took the boys in with it, too, but I let go and jumped back over the top.

When I was at the top of the wave, I saw Lisa. She was on my inner tube, and she was already out farther than she should have been. And she was still heading out, right for Mida Creek.

"Hey, Lisa! Leeeeesaaa!" I yelled. "Leeeesaaa!"

She never even turned around. Either the waves were too noisy or she was still mad at me. I looked back at the beach. Everybody was in the water; no one had seen Lisa.

"Mr. Barnes! Mrs. Barnes! Look at Lisa!" I yelled, but Mr. Barnes was trying to catch a wave with Sandy, and Mrs. Barnes was playing with the boys. Neither of them looked up. The waves were too noisy for them to hear me.

I looked out at Lisa again. She was already getting swept along, but she hadn't noticed because she was still heading out. If you're in a current in the water, you just go along with it. Unless you look up, you can't tell how fast you're going. *I can't just let her go!* I thought desperately. Without really thinking, I headed for her as fast as I could swim.

After a second I raised my head up and yelled at her again. I was already a lot closer, but now I was getting swept along, too.

"Lisa! Lisa Barnes!" I yelled. This time she looked up. "Come back! You're in Mida Creek."

"What?" she yelled. Then she looked around. Her face went white, and her eyes got really big. Then she started paddling like mad, splashing and kicking.

I looked back at the beach, too, and felt sick. We were already way out. For a second, I panicked and swam as hard as I could back toward land. I picked up my head to look, but I was even further out. I stopped and clamped my jaw to keep from screaming.

Think, Anika! I said to myself. *Daddy says that panic kills people. Think, even if you usually don't.*

I took a deep, sobbing breath and prayed, "Please help me, God! Please, in Jesus' name."

I turned around and looked for Lisa. She was still splashing like mad, further out than me. We'd be better off together, especially since she had an inner tube. I couldn't swim forever. I headed for her, aiming a little ahead and taking my time.

"Don't swim against a tide rip." It was almost like someone talked in my head. It was what Daddy had taught Sandy and me when we first started coming here. "Swim *across* a tide rip. Get out of the current."

OK, I thought. *As soon as I catch Lisa, we swim across.* I lifted my head for a look—almost there. I took a breath and kept swimming. *Stroke, stroke, breath.* Once I turned my head the wrong way and got slapped in the face by a wave just as I tried to breathe, but I kept on. *Stroke, stroke, breath. Keep kicking.*

Finally my hands touched the black rubber of the tube . . . and Lisa hit me over the head. I went down then bobbed up again, coughing and treading water.

"Get off! Get off!" she screamed. "You'll make it sink."

"What'd you do that for?" I demanded, but she was still screaming, not even listening to me.

I reached for the tube again, and she hit me again. I

was really tired. Boy, did I want to hang on and just let the tube hold me up. *I could just dump Lisa in the water,* I thought, and I almost fought with her. Then, *Think, Anika!* came into my head, almost like words.

I lay on my back and floated. We were out real far now, too far probably for the others to see where we were. *Well, if Lisa won't let me near the tube, I'll have to swim back to shore.*

"Go across the current," I yelled at her. "Swim across the current to the edge. This way!" Then, still lying on my back, I started kicking across the current, away from Lisa. She may look older than me and have sophisticated clothes, but she sure wasn't acting older now.

"Anika! Anika!" she screamed. "Don't go away. Help! Help!"

I sighed, lifted my head, and began treading water. "You have to share the tube then, OK?"

"OK! OK! Don't go away," she called.

"Promise you won't hit me again?"

"I promise! I promise!" she said. Then, when I was just finally reaching for the tube, she said, "Just be careful. Don't dump me. I'm scared."

"Me, too," I said, catching hold of the tube. For a second, I just hung there. It felt so good not to have to swim and get hit in the face with waves.

"Look! We're almost out to sea," Lisa said and started

kicking and splashing like mad again, which didn't get us any closer to shore.

It did, however, turn us over.

I grabbed the tube right away. Lisa just bobbed up and down splashing and yelling, so I kicked over to where she could grab the tube, too. She grabbed on and started crying really loud.

"Oh, I'm scared, I'm scared!" She howled, "I want to go home! I'm scared!"

"Lisa! Lisa! Stop it!" I said. She just kept right on, and finally I yelled at her at the top of my lungs, *"Shut up!"*

She did. Then in the quiet, I realized it was almost completely dark. The evening star was already out. It gets dark quickly near the equator. I started kicking across the current toward what I hoped was the nearest edge.

"Come on, Lisa, help me! We have to get out of Mida Creek," I said.

"What creek? This is the ocean, with sharks, too," she said and started moaning, "I'm scared, I'm scared!" again.

"This *current* is Mida Creek, you dummy," I yelled so she'd hear me. "We've got to get to the edge, so we can go back to shore. Kick!"

She kept on crying, but she started to kick. My legs

ached already, and the rubber of the inner tube pinched the skin under my arms where I was holding on. I was still kind of on the edge of the tube, so it was hard to make it go straight. Lisa was sitting in the tube.

It seemed like we kicked—and Lisa cried—for ages. In rhythm with my kicks, I kept praying over and over, "Jesus, help us. Jesus, help us." I was too tired and scared to think any more prayer.

Gradually Lisa stopped crying. For a little while all I could hear was the noise we made kicking. I couldn't keep kicking all the time anymore. I guess Lisa couldn't either, so the sound of our kicking kind of stopped and started again. In between and under it, I could hear the low roar that the ocean always makes. I couldn't tell which way we were going.

"Anika?" Lisa's voice sounded shaky in the dark.

"What?" My voice didn't sound any better. I stopped kicking to hear better and because I was so tired. Lisa stopped, too. We were shivering now. The water wasn't really very cold, but even in warm water you shiver after a while.

"You got caught in the current when you came after me, right?" Lisa asked through chattering teeth.

"Yes," I answered. It came out kind of jerky, like everything else we said.

"I'm sorry," she said.

I said, "That's OK. I guess I need to say I'm sorry, too, for trying to scare you and stuff."

We were quiet for a little while. The water was calm now. There were just stars and water, dark open space with no edges. I felt like I was floating in peaceful outer space. Everything seemed far away and odd.

After a while Lisa asked, "Why? I mean, why did you do all that stuff to me?"

I wanted to tell her that it wasn't all my fault and that I didn't mean to scare her at first. I wanted to ask her why she cried and whined all the time, but I didn't. It seemed like excuses all of a sudden.

Finally I said, "I guess I did it because I was scared about Daddy, and maybe because you're from the States and I didn't want to go there. But all I care about now is Daddy getting better. And doing what God wants, no matter what."

"Even if you have to go where you really don't want to be?" she asked.

"Yes, I guess," I answered. "Daddy said it's worth it even to die for Jesus. I guess it's silly for me to make such a big fuss about moving." Like a shock, I remembered where we were and added, "Especially now. We might not even be alive tomorrow."

Hearing myself say that scared me, and I started

kicking again. So did Lisa. She was still sitting in the tube, so she couldn't kick very well. I started praying again.

After a minute, I said, "Can we pray together and ask God to help us get back safe? I've been praying, but I'm still scared."

"I guess," Lisa said. "I don't know if he'll listen to me. I haven't hardly prayed at all since Mom and Dad decided to come here."

"Just say you're sorry, and he'll listen. Please?"

"Well, OK," she answered finally. "You go first."

"Dear God," I prayed, "please get us home safe. I said I'd do whatever you want, even go to the States, but I don't want to die yet. Please. In Jesus' name, amen."

Lisa was quiet for so long that I finally said, "Your turn."

"If I pray, do I have to say I'll stay in Africa if he wants me to?" she asked.

"I don't know," I said.

It was quiet again for a bit. Finally she started to pray. "Um, dear Jesus, please forgive me for being mad about being in Kenya and, um, being mad at Mom and Dad. Please let us get out of this safe. I'll try to like Kenya, I promise. Amen."

"You're supposed to say, 'in Jesus' name, amen,'" I whispered.

"In Jesus' name, amen," she said.

I felt like Lisa and I were all alone in the whole world, floating in a dark ocean in front of God.

"Friends?" she asked all of a sudden.

I smiled in the dark and said, "Friends!" and she reached over and squeezed my arm. That made the tube rock, so she quit.

We started kicking again, but finally I said, "I don't think it matters whether we kick or not, because I don't know which way we're going."

"It's silvery over there," Lisa said pointing. "It can't be morning already, can it?"

I looked, and she was right. I said, "It must be the moon. We'll be able to see which way to kick when it comes up. I think it's almost full because the tide was so high."

I was shivering so much the words came out hard. My mouth felt stiff and thick and slow.

We just lay there, watching. I was too tired and cold even to care. Once Lisa sort of slipped, but she was sitting in the tube so she couldn't fall out very easily. I woke up with a jerk when I slipped, and I grabbed on again. This time I hooked both arms over the tube, so it was kind of stuck under my arms and chin. I tried to kick again just to stay awake.

"Come on, we've got to hold on," I said, but it was

only a whisper. Lisa didn't answer. I yawned, then shook my head hard.

I had to stay awake, because if I fell asleep . . .

I shook my head again. I didn't even want to think about it.

Chapter
Nine

~~~~~~~~~~~~~~~~~~~~~~~~

I woke up when my face went under water. I kicked
hard to come up, and my foot hit a hard, sharp rock.
That really woke me up. I paddled, grabbed at the tube,
and missed.

My hands didn't work properly, and it was kind of
hard to move. I kicked toward the tube again and
banged my foot a second time. It hurt. Gradually it
sank in. The water was shallow. I could stand up. I did,
but it hurt my feet. Besides, I was dizzy. I wobbled and
lost my footing; my face went under again.

Finally, I was standing, balanced on a sharp piece of
coral. I looked around. The moon was all the way up, so
I must have really been out of it. I could see well in the
silvery light. Lisa was still in the tube, and it was drift-
ing away.

I looked again. Right in front of me, about ten feet
away, was a big stretch of coral reef sticking up out of
the water. It looked black in the moonlight. The tube
drifted up against it and stopped.

"Lisa!" I tried to yell, but my voice came out in a kind of a croak. The inside of my mouth was all shriveled up from the salt water. I swallowed and tried again.

"Lisa!" this time it was a sort of screechy whisper. She didn't even move. What if she was dead! Ugh. A violent shiver ran over my body, and then I couldn't stop shivering.

I had to get to her. I took a step. My foot slipped, and I bashed my shin on more coral. So I lay in the water and half paddled, half crawled to the tube. My arms still hurt, but they were working better. I guess they'd gone to sleep from being propped over the inner tube.

I tried to stand again. This time my feet hit sand. I could see the little patch of sand shining silvery white through the water. The moon is really bright at the coast in Kenya, and was I ever glad.

Lisa was still sitting in the tube, but her knees were just about touching her chin, like she'd almost slipped through and got stuck. Her head was hanging back, and her hair was trailing in the water. Her mouth was hanging open. She looked awful.

You can't drown if your head is out of the water, can you? I wondered. Everything felt odd and muddled. She couldn't be dead. I wouldn't let her be.

I grabbed her shoulder and shook her, but that just made her head wobble around. I tried to yell at her, but it still came out in a screechy whisper. I slapped her face hard, which made an explosion of pins and needles run up my arm. I hugged my arms to me. Lisa just had to wake up.

One of her arms moved, and she groaned. A wave of relief flooded my whole body, and I shivered even harder.

"Come on, Lisa. Wake up. Wake up!" Halfway through the second *wake up,* my voice came out really loud. I shook her shoulder and kept yelling.

Her eyes opened, and she tried to say something, but no noise came out. I grabbed her arms and tried to pull her out of the tube, but I couldn't. Somehow I felt like I just had to get her out. I yanked harder and the tube turned over. The water was only two feet deep. Frantically I tried to turn the tube back over. This time it came off.

Lisa thrashed in the water. I grabbed her hair and pulled her head up, then lost my balance and sat in the water beside her.

Lisa sat up, too, "Why did you do that?" her voice sounded cracked and scratched, too.

"Oh, you're all right," I said, relief washing over me. "Oh Lisa, I thought you were dead."

"I can't feel my legs," she sounded really scared.

"They're probably just asleep. My arms were," I

crawled toward the reef, cutting my knees when I got to the edge of the sand. I wanted out of the water. The coral wasn't so sharp on top of the reef, and I just kind of sat there for a second.

Lisa tried to stand up, yelled, "Ow, my legs!" and sat down again.

"Come on. Get out of the water," I said.

"I can't."

I looked back at her and realized that I could see the beach, too, about five hundred yards away.

"Look!" I called. "The beach! It worked. All our paddling worked. We got out of the current. We didn't get washed out to sea!"

Lisa twisted around and then really woke up. "All right!" she yelled. I was smiling so hard my cheeks ached.

The trees and stuff behind the beach looked black, but the white sand gleamed in the moonlight. A wave crashed on the other side of the reef. We were on the inside of the outer reef.

Suddenly, right in the middle of a laugh, I stopped dead.

"We've got to get out of here," I said and waded back toward Lisa. I'd just realized that the tide might be already coming in. "This reef could be under water in almost no time."

"At least we aren't out at sea," she said, and she tried to stand up again.

Just then, between me and the beach, I saw this light moving. I stopped and stared. Then it hit me: the African fishermen use lights to help them catch fish at night. An African fishing boat! A dugout canoe! And not very far away.

"Help!" I yelled like someone had yanked it out of my throat. "Help! Help! *Saidia! Saidia mimi!*"

I turned toward Lisa and screamed, "Yell! It's a boat."

She looked around wildly and fell down again. "Where?" she yelled, spitting out sea water.

"There," I pointed and yelled at it with my whole body.

The boat was turning, coming toward us. Now I could see a man standing, poling the boat along. I stopped yelling and felt dizzy. I wobbled and almost fell down, but didn't.

Just before he got to us, he called, "Jambo," like he'd just met us walking down the beach or something.

"Jambo," I answered him and just stood there like an idiot.

"Well, what is this affair?" he asked in Swahili, and I started bawling like a baby.

"Sorry, sorry," he said, but he sounded like he was almost laughing. He poled the boat closer and almost hit Lisa, who was still sitting down.

"My friend, my friend! Watch out for my friend," I said still sobbing. I felt stupid crying, but I somehow I couldn't stop.

Lisa tried to stand up again and fell. Her legs were obviously still asleep.

He got out of the canoe this time, and a smell of stale beer hit me. I couldn't believe it! He was drunk! He grabbed Lisa, picked her up, and dumped her in the canoe. Lisa had on sort of a skimpy bathing suit. Like I said before, Lisa was already pretty well developed—not like me.

The fisherman bent over her, leering at her. My stomach knotted up even tighter. "Stop it!" I yelled.

He turned around and laughed right in my face.

"Get in," he bellowed from about two feet away. Another sick smell of stale beer breath washed over me. I backed away.

"Get in!" he bellowed even more loudly and came toward me. I tried to dodge, but he grabbed my arm and shoved me into the canoe. His thin, tough hand bit into my arm, and he half lifted me over the edge. I bashed my shins on the side, then fell into the slimy water and fish scale stuff in the bottom of the canoe.

He picked up the pole and started poling back toward the beach.

I tried to sit up and banged my head on Lisa's knee

as she tried to get untangled with me. We ended up sitting jammed side by side in the canoe. I grabbed the edge with both hands and started to try to jump out. This fisherman didn't seem safe at all. *If I get away,* I thought, *maybe I can get help from someone else.*

Lisa grabbed me and held on. I kept trying for a second and then quit and just sat there. Lisa was right. I couldn't get away anyway; you can't run on coral in the dark with bare feet. And he'd just catch me if I tried to swim.

My whole body hurt. I looked at my legs and could see blood on them looking black in the moonlight. Lisa shivered next to me. The fisherman was still staring at her. It was warm out, but we were cold from being in the water so long.

I got my nerve up and asked the fisherman, "Where are you taking us?"

"To my house," he answered and leered at Lisa again. I glared at him.

"Who is your father that he would allow you to go out alone?" the fisherman asked suddenly, kind of sneering.

"My father is a good man," I answered indignantly. "We were swept away in Mida Creek."

"Where is the house of this good man, your father?" He said it really sarcastically.

I was supermad now. How dare he talk about my daddy like that? The air and wind on my wet skin made me shiver harder.

"What's he saying?" Lisa whispered. "I don't like this! Don't make him mad. You'll just make things worse." The fisherman and I had been talking in Swahili, so she could only tell what was going on by how things sounded and looked.

I hugged my knees and shivered. That fisherman thought we were asking for trouble. I mean, some of the people at the coast think any girl who is by herself is just asking for trouble—especially if she's not all covered up. But Lisa was right; making him mad wouldn't help.

I swallowed hard and tried to sound more polite when I answered, "My father is now staying at Bilge Water."

"I do not know that place," he answered. "You will stay with me this night," and he glanced at Lisa again.

"No, I will tell you where my father is," I answered. "You must take us there." Then I found out it wasn't so easy to explain where Bilge Water was. I didn't know where we were or how far the current had carried us. I tried to tell him from where the old mosque ruin was or from where you turn off the pavement.

He just kept saying, *"Sijui pale,"* which means, "I don't know that place."

This was real trouble. We were stuck with a drunk Swahili fisherman who had no intention of taking us home. As for the intentions he did have, well, I didn't even want to think about that.

"What's the matter?" Lisa whispered.

"He says he doesn't understand me when I try to tell him where Mom and Daddy are," I answered.

Lisa just looked at me and raised one eyebrow. "So what's he going to do with us?"

"He said we have to stay at his house—that's when he grinned at you like that. He's drunk, and he thinks we're sinful because we are by ourselves and not all covered up like his women."

"So what's the proper clothing for a girl to wear while getting washed out to sea, a snowsuit? Be real."

"I am being real, and I'm scared," I kind of snapped back.

I looked up at the fisherman right then. The steady clop and splash of him poling the canoe hadn't stopped, but now he was glaring at both of us. He looked angry.

Lisa followed my glance, swallowed hard, and said, "Maybe we should pray. I mean God answered our prayers last time—we're not out to sea or drowned." Lisa really was nice after all.

"Be still!" The fisherman's low voice spat the Swahili words out as if they were bullets. Just the look on his face made Lisa shut up for a couple of seconds, but she didn't understand what he had said and I didn't dare warn her.

A second later Lisa's cold hand reached for mine, and she started to whisper a prayer.

Whack! Ow! That hurt. Something cold had banged really hard on my shoulder. Lisa flinched, too. Then I realized the fisherman's pole had come down right where our shoulders were up against each other.

"What do you think you're doing?" he demanded. "I said to be still. Learn your place!"

The flash of anger I felt made me forget to be afraid or to think.

"What place is that?" I practically yelled at him. "Be careful, or your place will be jail."

He lifted the pole again and swung it at me. I tried to dodge, and then there was a terrific *thud* right inside my skull.

I must have been knocked out. Next thing I knew I was freezing cold, and my head was absolutely full of a terrible pounding ache. I could hear this moaning sound. After a second I realized it was me, so I stopped. I was lying on my back on top of something cool and gritty. I moved my hand . . . sand. I was on sand.

I opened my eyes, and a palm tree swayed back and forth in the moonlight. It all came back: Lisa, the drunk fisherman. Where was Lisa? I tried to sit up. That was a mistake. It was like my head exploded with pain. My stomach heaved, and I threw up.

I fell onto my back. The palm tree and stars were sliding sideways like things do when you've got a high fever.

I shut my eyes tight, and gradually my stomach felt better. Nothing happened. I couldn't hear anything at all except the low roar of the ocean and the wind.

"Lisa?" I called, but it didn't come out very loud, and the effort made my stomach tighten up again. Saying Lisa's name reminded me that she said we should pray.

"Dear God, please help. Please," I whispered. Nothing happened for a long time. I just lay there hearing the sea and the wind and feeling the cold sand. My thoughts were kind of slow and far apart. Gradually it sank in. If I hadn't done the same old thing—acted without thinking—I wouldn't be so sick now.

"Sorry, God," I whispered. "Please help me." All of a sudden, I felt as though he was right there with me somehow. "Please help Lisa, too," I whispered. I sure felt different about Lisa. I didn't even want to think about what might be happening to her.

The roar of the ocean had been getting gradually louder, but I wasn't paying attention. The tide was coming in, and I was on the beach.

I remembered how, once, when David had hit his head really hard, his mom hadn't let him go to sleep for ages. My muddled head knew there was supposed to be something bad about sleeping for people who'd been hit hard on the head. But it was so hard to stay awake.

Whack. Water hit the side of my head. That woke me up properly. I jerked, and my stomach twisted. *Whack.* Another wave hit me. It was getting to be high tide, and I had to move or drown.

I found that if I moved very slowly, my stomach would behave. Gradually I pulled myself onto my stomach and crawled up the beach. There's always a tangle of stuff on the beach at the high tide mark. Old coconut husks and driftwood hurt my cut knees, but I didn't quit crawling.

I flopped down on the powdery dry sand at the top of the beach. After a second I realized that opening my eyes didn't make me so dizzy anymore. I could even sit up if I moved very slowly.

I looked around. I was all alone on the beach. The fisherman's canoe was lying right at the edge of the water, looking like a big black blotch near the bottom of the sandy part of the beach. It was going to drift off with the tide pretty soon.

The moon was lower in the sky, but I could still see the tracks I'd made crawling up from the canoe. There were some other canoes out of the reach of the tide, not far from where I was sitting.

I realized I could hear people talking loud, arguing. The noise was coming from behind me, through some heavy bush. *Maybe that's where Lisa is,* I thought.

Without thinking I started to stand up to go to Lisa, but my dizzy head stopped me. After everything stopped whirling and my stomach decided not to throw up after all, I started to think—and pray.

"Please help me to do the right thing this time, God," I whispered. "Help me not to blow it again."

I could still hear people arguing. That is, I could hear angry voices, but I couldn't hear the words.

OK, I thought, *let's think this through properly. Lisa is up there, and if they're arguing about her maybe she's still all right.* Then I thought of something else: *Even if some of them want to help Lisa, she can't talk to them. She doesn't know Swahili.*

Finally I decided to go up quietly and try to see what was happening.

I was still kind of dizzy, but I could walk OK. I looked down, and there in the moonlight I could see where everybody else's tracks went into a gap in the bush.

That's where the path is, I thought. It would probably be better if I went through the bush, but I didn't think I could make it. I still felt very, very strange.

I walked along the edge of the path, hoping I wouldn't show up much in the moonlight. As I got closer, I saw that everybody was grouped outside one house, arguing and waving their arms. In the doorway of the house I could just see the fisherman who'd hit me. He was yelling at the others. Most of them had their backs to me, and the lamp in the house made their shadows stretch out toward me like huge, dancing black ghosts. I guessed that Lisa was probably in that house.

The people looked too busy to pay attention to me, so I stood up and walked normally. That was a lot easier on the head. But I'd forgotten something until a noisy yapping reminded me: there's always a few skinny yellow dogs hanging around any African village.

A couple of people on the outside of the circle turned to see what the dogs were barking at. It was too late to hide, and I couldn't run if my life depended on it. I just stood there kind of swaying on my feet.

One of the women screamed and pointed, then everybody swung around. They just stared.

"Jambo," I said. It was a silly thing to say, but I couldn't think of anything better. It came out really funny, too. Nobody answered. They just kept staring, so I started walking toward them.

All the women screamed and ran, and the men

backed up in a hurry. I'd never even thought that I
must look pretty weird by this time. I touched my face,
and my hand came away all sticky with half-dry blood
and sand. My hair was all sticking up, and my legs were
cut from the coral.

"Don't run," I pleaded in Swahili. "Please help me.
Where is my friend?"

Everybody kept staring, so I yelled in English, "Lisa!
Lisa, where are you?"

I heard a muffled sort of yell from the house, but it
was cut off like somebody had grabbed her mouth.

One of the women who'd started to run had come
partway back and was looking at me really hard. She
ducked into her house and in a second was back out,
running toward me with a cloth in her hands.

She stopped right before she got to me and hesitated,
"You are the daughter of Mr. Scott?" she asked with her
head to one side.

I nodded, and she wrapped the cloth around me, yelling something to somebody behind her. All of a sudden
it seemed like there were about twenty people crowding
around me, asking questions at once.

I felt really dizzy and just kept saying, *"Wapi rafiki
yangu?"* over and over, which means, "Where is my
friend?"

There was a loud argument outside the people

around me, and the next thing I knew Lisa was shoved through the people and standing next to me. I felt so relieved! Then, all of a sudden, I couldn't seem to keep my balance anymore. For the second time, everything went black.

Chapter
Ten

~~~~~~~~~~~~~~~~~

Something wet and cold hit my face. Somebody had
thrown water on me.

"Come quickly, come quickly," I heard vaguely in
Swahili, through the noise of people shouting.

"Anika! Come on!" That was Lisa.

I tried hard to wake up, but my head hurt so much.
Then hands grabbed me under my arms, yanking me
up and dragging me. I jerked my eyes open just in time
to see a man's silhouette looming out of the dark. The
sickening smell of stale beer washed over me. I wasn't
sure if it was a bad dream, but I wanted out of there.

I rolled over and frantically tried to get up. A huge
black arm swung over me and there was a loud *thwack*.
I cringed, but nothing hit me. I started crawling away
frantically, and my hand bumped a person's face. I went
around and kept going. There was a huge noise of
shouting behind me.

"Anika! This way!" That was Lisa's voice, just a little
to my left. I turned toward her and could see her

vaguely in the dark. A second later we stumbled through a door into an even darker house. A woman practically fell through the door after us.

It was hard to tell just from the moonlight through the door, but I thought it was the same woman who'd brought the cloth. How had she known who I was? Who was she? She shut the door, and it was pitch black in the house. I could hear her shove something across the door. When I peered through the dark at her, I saw she was holding onto her side, kind of bent over, and gasping.

There was still a lot of noise outside, but it was a bit muffled now with the door shut. I stayed where I was on my hands and knees on the floor, panting. I could hear both Lisa and the woman breathing hard.

Finally, I gasped out in Swahili, "Who are you?"

"Lydia, wife of Daudi," she answered between breaths. "I was at church. Your father gave us good words. I had to help you, but I don't know what my husband will do. He is not a Christian. Oh, what can we do?"

She gave a kind of gasp, and I heard her feet going away toward the back of the house.

It was dead quiet again inside. The noise outside seemed louder. I could hear the drunk fisherman bellowing and people arguing with him.

"Lisa? Lisa?" I whispered. I couldn't bear being all alone again and called out loud, "Lisa?"

"*Shhhh,* I'm right here," she whispered above my head. "Maybe they'll go away if we're quiet."

I felt around frantically in the dark and hit Lisa's foot. She sat down beside me, and we held on to each other. My head and legs hurt like mad, and I clenched my teeth to keep from crying. After a second I realized that Lisa might be hurt, too.

"Are you OK?" I whispered.

"Yeah, I guess," she answered. "Are you? I thought you were dead. You looked dead." She shivered and held on to me tighter.

"My head hurts, and so do my legs," I whispered. We held on to each other and listened. My head hurt like my skull was on too tight. I kept hoping to hear the woman come back, but there was only the noise of the argument outside.

I kept wondering about Lisa and what had happened. Finally I whispered, "What happened to you? Did he hurt you? I was afraid he would . . . ." I stopped.

"Yeah," she agreed, "I was scared, too. But what happened was really weird." She stopped and said slowly, "I guess God kept me safe, at least so far."

She didn't say anything else, and finally I couldn't stand it. "Well what *did* happen?" I blurted. Then I felt bad. "I mean, you don't have to tell if you don't want to."

"Oh, I don't care about that. It wasn't really terrible or anything—just weird. We got to the beach right after he hit you with that pole. You were just lying there like you were dead. He dumped you on the sand, grabbed me by one arm, and pushed me ahead of him up the beach. I was too scared to fight him after what happened to you.

"Anyway, this village or whatever it is was all quiet. He pushed me through a dark doorway and threw me on the floor. I rolled away from him and held still. Some woman came out of the back of the house with a lamp. When she saw me, she screeched and started yelling at him. He bellowed and waved his arms around. His back was to me. I heard a sort of hiss right behind me. Then somebody whispered at me, but I couldn't understand." Lisa stopped talking for a minute, then said, "If I ever get out of here, I'm going to learn Swahili."

She was quiet for so long that I finally said, "Somebody whispered?"

"Yeah, it was this really old woman. She had her head poked out of a door behind me. She was motioning me to follow her. You can bet I did, too. When I reached her, she shut the door and shoved something against it. Most of what happened after that was yelling.

The fisherman banged on the door and yelled. The old woman yelled at him and at me. The younger woman yelled and cried. . . . I think she's his wife or something. Can you imagine being married to that creep? Anyway, I just sat still and kept praying and praying.

"I guess the yelling woke everybody in the village, because pretty soon there were people outside the house yelling, too. It seemed like they kept on arguing forever, and I didn't know what they were saying. I figured out it had to be something about me, but I didn't know if that made it better or worse for me. The argument would get louder and softer, louder and softer.

"Then it all went quiet, and you yelled my name. I tried to yell back, but the old woman grabbed my mouth. She must have changed her mind, because all of a sudden she opened the window and practically shoved me out. A bunch of people grabbed me and pulled me to you."

"Did that fisherman chase you or something? Was that him who tried to hit me again?" I asked.

"He didn't hit you. He hit the woman who was helping you. He knocked her down, and you practically crawled right over her getting away."

"Oh. . . ." So that's whose face my hand had bumped when I crawled away. She'd helped me for no reason except that we were at church, and she'd been hit for it.

But that didn't stop her. I felt a huge bubble of thankfulness come up in me. What had she said her name was? L . . . L—something. Lydia, that was it—Lydia, wife of Daudi. And she didn't know what Daudi would think of what she'd done.

"Is this her house?" I asked.

"How should I know?" said Lisa. "It was the only house with a door open. She sure acted like it was. What'd she say to you anyway?"

"She said she's a Christian," I said. "Her name's Lydia, and she was at church where we were on Sunday. She helped us because of that. She's afraid of what her husband will do, though."

We were both quiet for a minute, and I realized that the shouting had stopped outside. I wondered again if this was Lydia's house, and if she would come back before her husband showed up. After a few seconds, I whispered, "We'd better pray."

"Yes," Lisa agreed like she really meant it.

"Dear God," I started, "Thank you that we didn't drown and that the fisherman didn't hurt Lisa. Please help Lydia's husband to help us get home."

"Yes," said Lisa. "Please let us get back to our parents, and let Anika be OK and her dad be OK, too. In Jesus' name, amen."

I hadn't thought about my dad all night, and a sick

feeling washed over me like a wave. It was too much. The back of my eyes ached, my throat felt hard and choked up. A sob came out. It sounded so loud it scared me, but suddenly I was crying, and I couldn't quit.

Thoughts swirled in my head, all mixed up. Lisa kept patting my shoulders and trying to get me to quit, but I couldn't. I kept thinking of things that just made me cry more—Daddy worrying; having to leave Kenya; being hurt and afraid in this dark hut; the smell of stale beer; Mom worrying about me; Lisa hating Kenya; us trying to scare the Barneses away (which seemed horribly mean now); the fisherman looming out of the dark over me; Lydia helping us even when she was hurt. . . . But the thought that kept coming back, and that hurt the most, was the thought of leaving Kenya.

Gradually I stopped crying so hard and got those hiccuping gasps you get after you've cried a long time. Now my head hurt even worse, but I had to admit I felt better inside. I sniffed and tried to wipe off my slimy face.

"Here," Lisa said and shoved a piece of cloth into my hand. "It was on the floor."

I'd just finished blowing my nose when stripes of light flashed across the room. A car had stopped right outside the house, and a second later another one pulled up. The second vehicle sounded like a Land

Rover. Lisa and I held perfectly still and listened. Doors slammed and loud feet stamped. There was a loud banging on another door, not ours, and a man yelled in Swahili, "This is the police! Open up!"

I was so busy listening to what was going on out front that I nearly jumped out my skin when I heard someone come in through the back of the house.

"Daughter of Mr. Scott? Daughter of Mr. Scott, are you here?" It was Lydia, and two other people were with her. What if one of them was her husband? I didn't answer.

A match flared, and I could see Lydia lighting a lantern. The people behind her were just dark blobs. Then the lamp caught, and I could see them. Two African men. One was a stranger who had a cloth around his middle and looked like a fisherman. But the other man . . . I was sure I knew him. But my mind wouldn't tell me who he was.

"It's the guy that preached," said Lisa, sounding really surprised.

Hasan? I thought and looked again. A smile started to grow on my face. Lydia had gone to get Hasan! I'd never even really noticed him before, not to see him as a person, anyway. He was always just one of Mom's African students. Now he looked familiar and safe. He could take us home.

"Hasan," I stammered and staggered to my feet.

"Oh, sorry, sorry," he said hurrying over to me and Lisa.

A tremendous banging on the door interrupted us. I'd forgotten all about the police out front. Lydia quickly went to pull back the table she'd shoved in front of the door and opened it.

The white edges of the policemen's eyes and the edges of their wide khaki shorts caught the light.

"You are hiding two white girls. You must give them up immediately!" one said.

"No." It was the other man who'd come with Lydia and Hasan who answered. "My wife was helping them. Juma was drunk and has beaten one of them. He found them on the reef."

"That's true," I blurted. "This woman is helping us." Lydia's husband wasn't so bad after all.

Both policemen swiveled to face me and Lisa, "You must come with us immediately!" the first one repeated. "You must make a statement."

My head throbbed, and I felt all dizzy again. I sure didn't want to go with those policeman—I was going to go home with Hasan.

"No," I said, "Hasan will take us home."

I should have known better. It's never a good idea to argue with police. If I'd just talked politely, I might have gotten somewhere. They simply stepped across the room, and one policeman grabbed each of us by the arm.

"Hasan, tell Mom," I yelled back over my shoulder as we were hustled into the back of the police Land Rover. They just left us there. There were no windows.

"You'd think *we* were the criminals," Lisa said, anger in her voice. "Let's get out of here." She rattled the door, but it wouldn't open.

"*Shhh*, listen," I said.

The police were telling Lydia that she'd have to come to the station. Then they started in on Hasan, saying he had to come, too.

"Oh no," I said.

"What's wrong now?" Lisa asked.

"The police are trying to get Hasan to come, too. If he comes, nobody will tell Mom and Daddy where we are."

"The police will, won't they?" she asked.

"Eventually, I guess." I just hung my head.

The front door of the Land Rover opened and slammed, and a second later we were moving. I didn't know if they'd taken Hasan and Lydia in the other car or not. I sure hoped they had that horrible drunken fisherman, Juma—or whatever his name was. I wanted him to get into lots of trouble!

That long bumpy ride into Malindi was one of the

166

worst rides of my life. Every jerk and jar of that Land Rover shot through my whole body. The seat was cold, and the sand on it hurt my bare legs. I ended up huddled against Lisa, crying.

She held on to me, trying to keep me from being joggled. She also kept talking to make me feel better, all about how God had kept us safe from the ocean and the fisherman. I really loved her then, but I still felt miserable and not safe at all. I wanted Mom and Daddy. Then I thought, *Daddy's so sick he couldn't take care of me anyway.* It just wasn't fair.

Finally the Land Rover stopped, and somebody opened the back.

"Get out," one of the policemen ordered in Swahili.

I just sat there. I hurt all over. Besides, I didn't want to make a statement, whatever that was, especially in Swahili. Until now, all my life, Daddy had done the talking whenever we had to do something with governments, banks, or official stuff.

"Get out," he ordered even louder and banged on the back of the Land Rover.

"What did he say?" asked Lisa.

"He said to get out," I answered.

"Well, let's do it then," she said climbing out. I followed her, moving slowly.

Lisa was already following the police onto the

veranda of the police station. Her hair was all tangled and sticking out, and she still just had a swimsuit on. That's all I had on, too, and I felt self-conscious going into a police station with just a swimsuit on. The bare light bulb above the door was the brightest light we'd seen all night, and it hurt my eyes as I followed slowly after Lisa and the police.

One policeman turned and looked back at me. He stopped dead in his tracks and stared. Then he burst into speech. It was too fast for me to follow—something about being hurt. Then he hurried back toward me saying, *"Pole, pole,"* which means "Sorry, sorry."

Two other policemen came out of the building, and they kept arguing with the first policeman the whole time they were taking me inside and making me sit down.

He kept saying over and over, "I didn't know she was hurt. It was dark."

Lisa stood beside me. I concentrated on sitting up straight. It seemed harder than usual somehow.

Vaguely I heard the door open and more people come in, but I didn't look up until Lisa yelled.

It was Mom! Mr. Barnes, Hasan, and Dr. Bishop were with her. I squealed, jumped to my feet, and tried to run to her. But my legs weren't working right, and I ended up doing more of a wobble.

Mom came toward me and caught me and took me right back to the chair. I landed in it just before I fell down. She held on to me and kept saying, "Anika, Anika," over and over. Every now and then she'd throw in a "Praise God."

I just put my head up against her and held on. Even the way she smelled made me feel safe. Then I thought of Daddy, looked up with a jerk that really hurt, and blurted, "Daddy's OK, isn't he? He's not worse?"

"Don't worry about your father," Mom said. "He felt much better as soon as we knew you were safe. Elsie Barnes is with him." She hugged me again. "We're just so glad you're alive."

Vaguely I heard Dr. Bishop, Hasan, and Lydia's husband talking to the police. Then Dr. Bishop came and looked at my head. He also made me look right at him so he could see my eyes and crouched down to look at the coral cuts. He did it all real quick, then went back to talking to the police. They seemed to talk for ages, but I didn't care because I was with Mom.

I was half aware that Lisa was talking and talking to Mr. Barnes, and part of me had room to feel happy that things were going to be OK between Lisa and her dad.

Next thing I knew, Mom was helping me out to a car. It turned out to be the Barneses' car. As we walked, I noticed it was getting light outside already. Lisa sat in front with her Dad. I sat in the back between Mom and Dr. Bishop. Dr. Bishop kept asking me about how I got hurt and what happened after. I was so sleepy I could hardly answer him.

Chapter
Eleven

~~~~~~~~~~~~~~~~~~~~~~~~~~~~~

I woke up when somebody was trying to pick me up out of the car. We were back at the house! I struggled to stand up and winced. Boy! Did it ever hurt!

"Now just you hold still, honey. We'll have you inside in a jiffy." It was Mr. Barnes. I could see his face and blue sky above him. Then I saw the doorway, then the ceiling, and then I was laid down on a bed.

"I guess our family has two down now, huh, Anika?" That was Daddy! I looked around wildly, and there he was, in another bed right across from me.

"I'm sorry, Daddy. I'm so sorry," I said. "I didn't mean to make you worry."

"It's just good to have you back," he said.

"Yes, and now we'd better see about getting her back to health." That was Dr. Bishop. "Now you take this pill, Anika. It will make things stop hurting so much and let me get those cuts cleaned up."

It felt so good to be at home, lying down, that even when Dr. Bishop cleaned out the cuts on my legs and head I didn't care. That pill must have been really strong, because I hardly even noticed when he stitched the cut on my head. Mom helped me out of my bathing suit and into pajamas. A second later I was fast asleep. Even the ice they put on my head couldn't keep me awake.

I kind of half remembered Dr. Bishop waking me up a bunch of times during the night and making me look at a light. It must have been OK because he let me go back to sleep again. Actually, I don't think I would have stayed awake no matter what they did. I could have slept on the back of a galloping camel.

Nothing mattered except that the whole crazy adventure was over, and everything was OK now.

What I didn't know as I drifted off to sleep was that I was wrong—the adventure wasn't through with me yet.

I guess I slept all day and the next night, too. When I finally woke up, it was just starting to get light outside and the birds were singing. I looked over at Daddy. He was still asleep, and there was nobody else in the room. My head and legs were aching, but not near as badly as before. I lay there feeling warm, sleepy, and happy.

I thought about going back to the States, and it didn't scare me as much as before. If God could keep us from dying in the ocean and get us safely away from that fisherman, he'd take care of me in the States. It wasn't like I wanted to go, but it was really OK now.

I wondered if that's how Lisa felt about staying in Kenya now, and I decided to ask her when I got the chance.

A movement caught the corner of my eye, and I turned my head just in time to see Mom looking in. She saw me and came to lay her hand on my forehead. Her hand felt really good, cool and comfortable, when she ran it over my forehead, below the cut.

"Feeling better?" she asked.

I nodded and said, "My head and legs still kind of hurt, though."

She went out for a minute and came back with a glass of water and some Tylenol, then helped me sit up to take it. I didn't really need help, but I liked her arm behind me.

"I'm glad you're feeling better, Anika, because you've got some decisions to make today," Mom said.

"I already decided that it's really OK with me if we go back to the States," I said, adding, "even if we have to stay there."

"That's super, Anika, but that's not what I'm talking about. Lisa has said that she doesn't want to press charges against the fisherman who brought you in from the reef. Since you were hurt the most, we've agreed to let you decide."

"She wants to let him just go free?" I said. I could hardly believe my ears. "Why?"

"You'll have to talk to her about that. You pray about it. I'll go get you some breakfast."

When she said that I suddenly realized I was practically starving to death. I called, "Pancakes, OK?" just as she disappeared through the door.

I'd said it loud without thinking, and that woke Daddy up.

"Good morning, sheep," he said.

"Sheep?" I asked. "Why sheep?"

"Rejoice for the lost has been found," he said and grinned at me.

He meant that I was like the lost sheep in Jesus' story. That sheep had gotten lost because it had been stubborn and silly. It wandered away from the other sheep and didn't come when the good shepherd called it.

"Shouldn't I have gone after Lisa?" I blurted. "Was that wrong?"

"I don't think so, Anika," Daddy said. "I didn't mean you were disobedient, just that we were very glad to find you."

It was kind of embarrassing to talk about me, so I

changed the subject. "Are we going back to the States right away?" I really wanted to know.

"As soon as we can get packed and book a flight," Daddy said. "But I'm hoping we won't have to stay long. If the tests for complications are clear, we should be able to come back so your mom can teach next term at the Bible school. I'll have to rest," he said, making a silly, sad face. Then he added, "I think I'll have the discipline to do it now."

"Discipline to rest? I don't get it," I said. "Resting is easy."

He just laughed and said, "Not for me, it isn't, but I think I've learned that sometimes God has harder things for me to do than running around and getting work done." He paused and added, "'They also serve who only stand and wait.' I've known that all my life, but never understood it. I guess it's my turn to wait on God and to rest."

All of a sudden a verse came into my head, and as usual I blurted it right out. "They that wait upon the Lord shall renew their strength. They shall mount up with wings like eagles; they shall run and not be weary; they shall walk and not faint." I smiled. It was almost like a promise that God would make Daddy better. Daddy smiled, too, so for once, talking without thinking didn't get me in trouble.

Just then Mom came in to ask me if I wanted to get up for breakfast. "Dr. Bishop said it would be all right if you wanted to get up."

I looked over at Daddy, but he just shrugged and said, "I'll be staying in bed to practice my waiting, but I don't think that's your job right now."

Mom said, "Waiting?" and looked real puzzled. When Daddy laughed and said, "Just something Anika helped me to see," I felt great all over, even if a few parts did hurt.

"I feel great," I said. "Sure, I'll get up."

A few minutes later, I wasn't so sure. Ow! Was I ever sore, and my head hurt when I stood up. I put my hand on my head, and my hand hit this horrible, stiff, yukky, stringy stuff. My hair! gross! Suddenly I realized that I was sticky with itchy salt.

"Mom, can I take a shower first? Yuk! I'm filthy."

Mom checked with Dr. Bishop, and he said it would be OK, but not to soap the scraped and cut places or the stitches. In the shower, a bunch of old blood came out of my hair, and a bunch of hair, too. I didn't know what all the hair was from until I looked in the mirror.

Dr. Bishop had shaved a patch of my hair off right above my forehead when he put in the stitches. The bare spot had three gross black stitches in it. It was all green and purple and blotchy, and so was my forehead.

I looked like Frankenstein.

I just stared for a second and said, "I want to go lie down."

"OK, Anika, come on out for breakfast when you feel like it. It's not quite ready yet, anyway," Mom said as she helped me back to bed.

"Can't you bring it to me?" I asked. "I mean, I look really gross."

"It won't do you a bit of good to hide, Anika," she answered and left.

I sat on the bed and looked at my legs sticking out from my shorts. The whole front of my shins were covered with big scabs and bruises from the coral. I pulled the sheet over them so I couldn't see them.

"Anika, for someone who had enough sense to get two people out of Mida Creek, you're acting very silly," Daddy said quietly.

"You don't understand!" I said and huddled under the sheet to pretend to be sleeping.

The smell of breakfast floated through the door, and my mouth watered like mad. I was starving. Mom brought Daddy a plate of pancakes. I pretended to be sleeping, but I could hardly stand it.

I thought I might get my way when Mom said softly, "Maybe I was too hard on her. Look, she's sleeping again."

Daddy's chuckle ruined everything. "I wouldn't give up on her just yet," he said. He knew I wasn't sleeping.

I finally had to get up and go out. It was either that or starve.

It was just as bad as I thought. Everybody stared at me like I was from Mars. I had just sat down at the table when it hit me. I was going to have to go to the States looking like this! Dad said we were going right away. I would look like a cross between a zombie and a victim of the chain-saw massacre.

That fisherman, Juma, or whatever his name was, would pay for this!

My pancakes didn't even taste all that good after that horrible revelation. *Watch out U.S.A., here comes Frankenstein Anika Scott,* I thought and put my head down. I was not going to cry! Everybody was already staring at me. I swallowed hard, lifted my head, and put a fork full of pancake into my mouth.

David and Alex were really staring at me, almost as if they were scared. They were sitting together, and whenever I looked at them it was like looking at two bug-eyed lizards. I made a face at them, and David giggled. I frowned. *I feel like a freak show!* I thought in disgust.

"How come that fisherman hit you so hard?" asked Sandy.

"Shh!" said Traci, "maybe she doesn't want to talk about it."

"Well, I want to know," Sandy insisted. "I'm sick of people not talking about what happened at the village, or how they got to the police station. Anika isn't paranoid like Lisa. She's not the one whose fault it was that they got swept out to sea. I'm tired of people not wanting to talk about it."

So Lisa hasn't told them anything about the fisherman, I thought, just as Mom interrupted Sandy. "That's enough of that!" she said.

I glanced at Lisa to see how she felt, but she was looking down so I couldn't see her eyes. It seemed really weird to think that only a couple of days ago I'd have agreed with Sandy about Lisa being paranoid. Now I knew different. Lisa was great, but I still wondered why she hadn't told. Maybe it had something to do with not wanting to charge the fisherman. Well, I wanted him to get everything that was coming to him and even more. Just look what he did to me! Also, I didn't want to be called paranoid for not telling.

"Is it OK if I tell?" I asked Lisa. She just kind of shrugged and looked at me like she wanted to say something. But she didn't.

I guessed that didn't mean no, so I started, "You know we got swept out to sea and landed on the reef?" I asked. They nodded. "Well, this fisherman picked us up, but he was drunk. I hate him! He stared at Lisa and wouldn't listen when I tried to tell him where we lived. Then he said I didn't know my place and hit me with the huge pole he was using to push the canoe along. I hope he ends up in jail forever!"

"But Anika . . ." That was Lisa. She had never talked at the table before unless somebody made her, so I was surprised. Besides, I thought she shouldn't like that fisherman any more than I did. Wasn't she my friend now?

"But what?" I demanded.

She just looked down again and said, "Oh, nothing."

"I think Lisa would like to talk to you by yourself after lunch," said Lisa's dad, talking too loud. It didn't bug me as much as usual. He'd been great last night. *Uncle Joey?* I thought. It sounded odd, but kind of nice. Uncle Joey.

Nobody wanted to talk about the fisherman anymore, but Sandy and Traci kept asking me about getting out to the reef. I guess Lisa had told them I was a hero because I knew to paddle to the edge of the current. That made me feel good, but kind of silly, too.

By the time breakfast was over, I was getting dizzy again and wanted to go lie down. Mom got me to lie down on my bed in my old room this time. I guess that was so Lisa could talk to me, because she came in a few minutes later.

She sat down on her bed and looked at me. Then she looked down and twisted her hands together. She looked nervous.

"Are you all sore still? I mean do you have a bunch of bruises and stuff from that night?" I asked just to say something.

"Not like you, but some. See?" She pulled up her T-shirt sleeve and showed me a bruise that looked like finger marks on the top of her arm. "That's where that fisherman grabbed me, and I've got some scrapes on the back of my legs from where I kept falling down in the coral."

"I hate that fisherman!" I blurted.

"But—but . . . ," she said again like she did at breakfast, and then she kind of blurted, "What if those people get to be bitter against Christians if we make him go to jail? What if it gets Lydia and her husband in trouble with the whole village for helping us?"

"So?" I demanded, "What if it does? God said an eye for an eye, and that man hurt us."

"But we read about Jesus on the cross last night at devotions when you were still asleep. Jesus even forgave the people who killed him. Dad said he even took the punishment for their sins, too. I just thought—"

"Lisa! I thought you were my friend," I interrupted, practically yelling. It made my head hurt. "Look what that horrible man did to me, and you want to let him go free? I have to go to the States looking like Frankenstein because of him, and you want me to just say that's OK?"

Getting really mad nearly always makes me start to cry, and it did then. It wasn't fair! I turned over and ignored Lisa, hoping she'd go away and not notice I was crying.

She didn't go away, and she knew I was crying, too, because she patted my back, which I hate. When she started talking, I stuffed my pillow over my head, so I didn't hear the first bit when I was moving, but the rest came through anyway, ". . . inner tube we prayed to obey God, and he *did* keep us safe and stuff," she was saying. "I mean, Jesus loved me even though I was hating Kenya. It's hard to say it right, but doesn't God love that fisherman, too? I mean, shouldn't we forgive him, too— turn the other cheek and all that? I thought maybe we could not make charges. Then we could tell him it was because we're Christians and Jesus loves him."

She sat there a minute more, then when I wouldn't come out she finally left.

That's when I really did cry. Every sob hurt the stitches on my head and reminded me what I looked like. I knew Lisa was probably right, and that made me even madder. I stuffed the pillow over my face so nobody would hear, and it got all gooey. My mouth tasted of salt, and I was so, so mad. I must have gone to sleep, because the next thing I remember is waking up with my eyes all sticky and my head hurting.

There were tiny spots of bright sun on the walls where the light came through the thatch, and it was hot. I rubbed my eyes and remembered that I had a decision to make. Just remembering made me mad all over again, but I couldn't quit thinking about what Lisa said about Jesus forgiving the people who killed him.

That doesn't count, I argued in my head. *He knew he was going to come alive again.* It was almost like Jesus was in the room just looking at me like he was sad. I didn't want to, but I remembered the verse, Isaiah 53:5, that we had learned for the Easter musical: "He was wounded and bruised for our sins. He was beaten that we might have peace; he was lashed—and we were healed!"

I was still lying on my back, looking at the thatch. Tears ran down over my cheeks and into my ears. "OK, OK," I said right out loud, "I'll do what Lisa said."

It was just like a big stone lifted off my chest. I guess Mom had heard me talking, because a second later the door opened and Mom asked, "Did you call me, Anika?"

"No," I said, "but I need to talk to Lisa."

183

Mom looked back into the big room behind her and called Lisa, then went out. A second later Lisa came in. She sat on the bed and just looked at me.

"I decided," I said. "We can do like you said. I didn't want to, but I kept remembering what you said about Jesus loving us even when we were bad. I guess he even loves that fisherman."

Lisa smiled this huge smile and hugged me. Just then we heard the *flap-slap* of running thongs on the porch and David giggling.

"I guess everybody is back from the beach," said Lisa. "We can tell them."

Mr. Barnes's voice boomed, "Lisa! Lisa! Come here!"

Uncle Joey, I thought, and I grinned. He sure was noisy, but he was OK.

Lisa wrinkled up her nose and started to get up.

I just had time to ask really quick, "Is it OK for you about staying in Kenya now?"

She nodded just before she went out the door.

I'd just sat up and was getting ready to go out, too, when Mom came in and sat down by me. "Are you feeling better?"

"Uh huh, I guess," I said. "We decided not to charge that fisherman with anything, but I'm still scared about going to the States—especially looking like this." I touched my green and yellow bald spot.

184

"Oh, honey," Mom said and squeezed my hand. "I'm sorry. We should be able to do something with your hair to cover most of it."

That made me feel better. Not great, mind you, but better. When I went out with Mom, Uncle Joey didn't help much by booming out, "Well, look who's here! Our little Anika, and she carries the honorable wounds of a hero. They're pretty colors, too!"

He bellowed with laughter, but nobody else laughed, and I saw Aunt Elsie kick him under the table. He took another look and said, "I'm sorry, Anika. I guess that was uncalled for."

He looked so sorry I just had to smile. He really was OK. "I'll survive, Uncle Joey," I answered. And I knew I would, too.

"'Uncle Joey,' is it? That sounds good," he said, and he looked so happy it made me happy, too.

Later on, I was outside sitting on the porch. I looked all around, trying to memorize everything I saw. My heart sank as I wondered what it would be like in the States.

"It's a good thing you're going with us, God," I said, right out loud. "At least there will be someone there to help me get used to things."

I looked around again. It wasn't going to be easy. I knew that. But at least I wasn't alone.